KING OF ASH

AVA MASON

PROLOGUE

Everyone is born with a purpose in this life. I've always known that. As soon as a person takes their first breath, they are endowed with a meaning, a quest. It is what defines them, what drives them. For twenty-one years, I thought I knew what that was for me.

Then, everything changed.

Now I know that purpose. Her.

The woman I'm meant to live for and the one for whom I would lay down my life.

1

Stryder

I leaned in to Kip's ear, my voice a growl but trying to remove as much emotion as I could so she could understand the instruction.

"Let Thunder take you. He will keep you safe. I'll call for him when I am done."

I had no more spoken the last word when I pushed myself up and off the great beast's back. My wings caught a stream of air and I pushed upward, bending my body backwards so that I flipped in mid-air. Ominous Thunder roared toward the tree line, taking Kip with him. She looked back to me, her mouth agape as she saw me soaring through the air for the first time. In spite of the danger, I felt like showing off, and dove toward the first of the Bogles I saw.

I tackled him mid-stride, and we tumbled to the ground together. His wide, thick body struggled to regain his footing, and I pounced on him, laying my fists into his soft underbelly. He grabbed one of my wings and began to pull, either to rip it or to pull himself up, and I unsheathed the sword from my hip, slicing in one motion, and spilling his guts onto the ground.

The smell of his blood splattered on my body awoke the war inside of me. The stench of his skin, already beginning to rot under the sun, and my hand wiping away the warm thick blood from my face, brought back the instinct of battle, and I spun on my heel, jabbing my sword into the throat of another Bogle. He gurgled and spittle ran down his jaw, mixing with his plasma, his momentum carrying him a few more steps before his body collapsed.

I took a few running steps and leapt into the air, my wings catching me and sending me higher again. The pain in my leg from the poisoned cut was a burning reminder of the danger these goblins posed. They were dumb, and fought without any seeming strategy, but they were vicious and cruel. Entire clans had been hacked to pieces by them, and what they lacked in strategy, they made up for in numbers and a willingness to take damage to deal damage.

From my vantage point in the sky, I could see Roane dealing with two of them. He had also sent his horse away, carrying Harley with him. In the distance, I could see the two powerful animals slowing down their pace, their instincts telling them they were far enough from danger, but their loyalty not letting them get any further from us. Roane looked up to me and shouted something, but I couldn't make it out. Just a second later, a white hot burning roared through my body and I began to tumble from the sky.

I landed hard on the ground, the flaming arrow still sticking into one wing, and I scrambled to my feet. The Bogle archer was charging me, and I yanked the arrow out of me and tossed it aside. Blood trickled from the white feathers, and I winced as I tried to move it. The Bogle was close enough for me to smell his odor and I slid to the ground, sticking up my foot into his stomach and reaching up. I grabbed his head as he bent over my kick and pulled as I shoved his body up and backward, sending him barreling above and behind me. He landed with a thud.

As he tried to stand, I slammed my sword into his hand, pinning him down to the ground. His scream of pain filled the air and I kicked into his jaw, shutting his mouth and silencing his scream with unconsciousness. A thrust downward of my sword into his throat silenced it forever. A blow from behind me shoved me forward and I spun to face the lead Bogle. His sword was already slicing through the air and I ducked, rolling away from it.

My sword swept through the air on instinct, trying to find purchase with his legs, but he moved just in time. Sweeping up in an arc, my sword met his and clanged loudly. He thrust forward wildly, and I parried it, allowing him to stumble toward me. Pulling my sword in, I lifted it up and shoved with my entire weight. As his face came within inches of mine, I could see his features drop as the blade cut through the bottom of his jaw and up into his brain. It exited through the top of his skull and he slumped into me, forcing me to abandon my sword and fall away.

Roane came running to me and helped me stand as we surveyed the scene. Five dead Bogles and a river of goblin blood surrounding us, our bodies matted with it, our swords buried deep in their tissue and our wings charred or bloody from their mindlessly violent attacks.

War never changes.

"You're hurt," Roane said, coming toward me.

There were slashes through his clothes and blood spattered on his face, but it was hard to tell how much of it came from him and how much of it belonged to the creatures now scattered at our feet. The fight had battered me, but his eyes were locked on the first injury I'd sustained when facing the goblin horde. As if acknowledging it made it real, the slice through my leg started to burn.

"The first one got me with his knife," I told him.

"You need to get the poison out," Roane said.

I shook my head. "No. We need to get Kip to the court as fast as we can. There's no time."

"And if you don't get that cut taken care of, you won't have any time at all. You won't live long enough to get her to the Blood Court."

The sound of hooves announced Ominous Thunder and Aramis racing back to us. We hadn't called for the horses, but they had been alongside us in enough battles to sense when they were needed. Kip clung to Thunder with a look of terror in her eyes and flung herself down as soon as the horse stopped. At least, I hoped she'd done that herself and hadn't just fallen off. The landing wasn't smooth either way.

But she didn't seem to care. She was too focused on the blood trickling down my leg from the poisoned cut.

"We need to get him some help," Roane said.

Kip reached into the bag she'd brought with her through the portal and pulled out a T-shirt. In one swift movement she tore the fabric into a long strip and bent down to wrap it around my leg. I reached down to stop her.

"Let it bleed," I told her. "It will help get the poison out of my body."

Climbing up onto Ominous Thunder, I reached down for her and swung her up behind me again. Her head buried down into my back and I knew she was doing everything she could to avoid looking at the bodies of the Bogles on the ground or the blood turning the dirt to mud beneath us. I urged my horse toward the forest, hoping I'd find the help I needed and would be able to see this through.

Kip's arms wrapped tightly around me and her soft, warm body pressed against mine gave me the strength to push past the pain and the burn of the poison. It told me I could get this done.

2

*K*ip   If this was a movie, after Stryder pulled me up onto the back of the glistening black horse, it would have taken off at a slow, but impressive trot to make sure the full drama of the moment sank in. It would be the perfect time for one of those big, sweeping shots that started just on the cut in his leg and pulled out until it showed the carnage around us and then the land stretching out on all sides. Eventually, when the two of us and the horse underneath were barely visible against the landscape, the animal would take off and run into the distance.

This was not a movie. Which was why there was no buildup, no chance for me to process what was happening. Instead, the animal had taken off running like his tail was on fire and I had to adhere myself to Stryder's back to keep from tumbling off. That would have brought this entire journey to an unfortunate and exceptionally unpleasant end.

Not that this had been the most pleasant of trips so far. I'd decided to push the images of the fight I'd just witnessed into the furthest back corner of my mind and just let it sit there.

That was too much for me to deal with on top of how worried I was about Stryder. 'Let it bleed' wasn't something I wanted to hear come out of his mouth after a warning about the poison in the knife. Not only did it flagrantly fly in the face of the four-hour first aid training course I took last summer when I briefly contemplated life guarding, but it also meant the risk might be more severe than I wanted to think. It wasn't just another cut or puncture, not just another wound sustained during yet another battle.

I clung to him as tightly as I could, pressing my face into his back to stop the sting of the wind whipping against my face as the horse ran. What did he call him? Ominous Thunder? Really? That was going to warrant a conversation later when I wasn't worried that Stryder was going to die in front of me. The animal felt like it was getting faster the farther we went. Its feet pounded into the ground so hard I could feel the vibrations going up through my body.

"How in the living hell did I get here?" I muttered to myself.

I knew, of course. The entirety of the last few days wasn't lost on me. Neither was the fact that technically, technically, I was here of my own accord. Coming to the Land of the Sidhe with Stryder and Roane had been my choice. But if there had ever been a choice made under duress, I'd say that was one of them. Agreeing to go with them was a compulsion that stemmed from the pain I felt at losing Mac. His death was more painful than anything I'd experienced since losing my parents, and the shock of how it had happened only underscored the sadness.

After witnessing that brutality, I wanted to do something, anything, to avenge my dear friend. And that led to me sitting astride a horse – something I'd never done – latched desperately to the back of someone I didn't even know if I could trust. The revelation about why Stryder had come to Glendale ruined everything. All that had built up between us, all I thought we were starting to feel, was gone the second those men confirmed he had been there to kill me.

He had been there for me. He'd protected me and ensured the Summer Queen's men didn't get me in their clutches. His trusted advisors had sent him to kill me so I couldn't help her, but he had chosen not to do it. Even though he had every opportunity. That dagger would have made quick work of me. He could have run me down while I was walking across the parking lot at the convenience store. With his size, it probably wouldn't have been hard for him to just snap me into little travel-size pieces if he wanted to.

Running inventory on the ways Stryder could have snuffed me out didn't do wonders for my confidence. I didn't know what to think about him or what was happening. When I was brave enough to peek away from his back, the world around me was stunning. When I was able to look beyond the horror that stained it, the beauty was indescribable. It was like wandering into the drawings of one of the books on Mac's shelves. After a few moments, it sank in that it was exactly like those drawings because those drawings were of this place.

The fear of imminent tossing and trampling wasn't a match for the glorious surroundings. I lifted my head away from Stryder and looked around to take more of it in. But the longer I looked, the more I noticed the signs of violence. Shattered trees and tamped grass matted in blood created a horrific path along one side. Bits of cloth scattered across the ground made me not want to think about the jagged white shards nearby.

Finally, the pace of the horses slowed enough to let me breathe again. I sat up straighter and looked behind me to check on Roane and Harley. I half-expected her to be hanging on to the horse's tail rather than Roane. Clinging to a hero wasn't exactly her style. Instead, she had her arms tight around his waist and her hands gripping the front of his shirt. As soon as she felt the horse beneath her slow, her grip lessened, and she looked around Roane toward me. One hand lifted away from Roane to flash me a thumbs-up.

There's the Harley I know.

Stryder held back on Thunder until Roane was able to catch up with us and ride alongside.

"Where are we going?" Roane asked.

"We'll go to Minerva and Valerie," Stryder said. "Minerva will have what I need to take care of the cut. While we're there, Kip and Harley can change clothes and we can pick up some supplies."

"I'm actually pretty comfortable," Harley said. "Why do we need to change clothes?"

Leave it to Harley to just skip past that whole mortal wounding thing. She was worried about losing her style.

"You want to be able to blend in as much as possible. There isn't a whole lot of human tourism around here," Roane said. His voice dropped just slightly. "It will keep you safer."

The deeper they brought us into the woods, the more I felt the heaviness of our surroundings. Fear pricked the back of my neck and the feeling of being watched crept along my skin. Stryder tensed and I worried he was feeling the same thing. Relief flooded me when we reached a clearing and I saw a small cottage a few feet away. It was barely noticeable against the backdrop of the woods. The thatched roof blended with the hanging moss and the walls blurred to look like more trees. All that stood out was a chimney made of smooth river stones sending a thin tendril of purple smoke into the air and the glistening brass handle on the narrow front door.

Stryder dropped down off his horse and led it a few more steps toward the cottage.

"Minerva," he called, his voice rough. "Are you there?"

Seconds later the tiny house cracked open and the front door sank back so a woman in a flowing lavender gown could step out.

"Stryder, what are you doing here?"

The question faded on her lips when her eyes fell on the gash in his leg.

"Bogles," he told her. "It's poison."

Her eyes flickered to Harley and me. Without another word, she gestured for us to come inside. The look on her face didn't inspire a sense of security and reassurance in me. There was a lot less 'Come on in, we'll have cookies and milk while I fix that right up, then you can go on your way' and more 'Well, fuck. If you're going to die, you might as well do it in here where the birds won't peck at you.' Since I was expecting Harley and me to be the big conflict at this moment, I was not encouraged by her total focus on him. The feeling made my stomach lurch with anxiousness. I couldn't handle another death, not now and not *his*, even though I wasn't entirely sure I could trust him.

Stryder reached up for me and helped me to my feet. I couldn't help but notice the shaking in his arms as I got to the ground. The poison was moving rapidly through his body, weakening him so that he went from being able to toss huge creatures around to barely being able to hold me up. I watched him carefully, worried he would fall over at any moment.

Harley swung her leg over Aramis's back and tried to fling herself to the ground, but Roane caught her. He held her close to himself for a bit longer than might have been strictly necessary, but she didn't protest.

We rushed into the house and a younger woman appeared toward the back of the first room.

"Valerie, bring these two and freshen them up," the woman Stryder called Minerva instructed. "And get my utensils heating in the fire."

That was a request I wished I hadn't heard.

"Thank you," Stryder said.

The younger woman nodded slightly toward us and turned

away. Harley and I followed her out of the room as Minerva approached Stryder intensely.

"What are you doing, Stryder?" she hissed as she started tearing away at his pants to reveal more of the injury. "Going head to head with the Bogles."

"They were camped out near the portal. I had no choice."

He growled and I could only imagine whatever the woman was doing hurt.

"And them? Do you realize how dangerous this could be for us?"

"I know, Minerva. It's only for one night. They just need to get acclimated to being here."

I didn't hear anything else because Valerie ushered us the rest of the way down a hallway and into another room, closing the door behind her. I was glad for that. Utensils warming in a fire could only mean one thing and that was something I didn't want to witness.

"The bath is behind that curtain," she told us. "I'll find you more appropriate clothing."

Harley gave me a sideways look as we made our way toward the bath. The idea of washing away everything that had happened since we escaped the Fae men was wonderful.

"I don't think I like the welcoming committee very much."

3

Stryder

"Why are they here, Stryder? They wouldn't need to be acclimated to our world if you hadn't brought them here," Minerva asked forcefully.

It was a genuine question, but I knew full well she was asking it as much to distract me as she was to get the information. The poison from the Bogle's blade was coursing rapidly through my veins and if she didn't get it out of me and absorb what was there fast enough, it could kill me. That meant the use of heated metal utensils and rare herbs not designed to comfort. It was a process I didn't relish.

"They're here because they need to be," I told her.

She'd started examining the wound when I was still standing in the living room, but now I'd moved back into the small room to the side of the cottage and stretched out across a wooden table so she could more easily do her work. This was a room she never wanted anyone to find. Much like many of the other things she did, using these herbs and performing the procedures she did was not looked at kindly, especially for someone who had been cast out of the court. But there were many lives in the

Sidhe that were owed to her not being willing to live by the guidelines and demands of others.

In most ways. Her willingness to resist applied to using forbidden plants and performing surgeries, but it faded some when it came to having two human women in her home. Especially two human women accompanied by the targeted King of the Blood Court.

"I need more than that if you're going to have them under my roof. Even for one night," she said. "Spies from the North have been sniffing around here and I don't need any more focus brought to me. I need more than just you saying they need to be here."

"I need more, too," Roane said.

He stepped up beside Minerva, my best friend standing beside the oldest friend of my mother. There were so many similarities between the two. Both treasured confidants of the Blood Court. Both driven from their homes. For Roane, brought out after the rest of his kingdom was wiped out so he could be raised and protected within the Blood Court. For Minerva, sent into exile during the same horrifying conflict, forced away from the court to save herself and those she cared about the most.

"Even you don't know what he's up to?" Minerva asked, reaching for the handle of one of the tools sitting in the flames.

I felt like she was preparing to scold me for some boyhood prank, but might be a little softer on me considering what I was about to go through.

"There wasn't time to tell him everything."

I braced myself.

"But there's time now," she said.

I cringed and hissed against the pain searing through me as she cut into my skin around the wound. Kip was too close for me to let out the scream building in my throat. It would frighten her and I didn't want to do that.

"No," I finally managed when the pain eased enough to speak. "You're right. We have to keep going. There's no time to stop now."

Minerva put the tool back into the fire and took up another one. Her head was shaking even if her eyes were still filled with concern.

"No. You were right to come here. You have to be safe. Two human girls with no sleep and empty bellies aren't going to be any help to you. You'll stay for dinner and rest for the night. Tomorrow you go on your way."

"I don't want to put you in any more danger than I already have."

"You're already here. I'm not going to let you leave when you still need to recover and those women aren't ready for travel. It will be making the situation far worse than it already is."

I knew she was right. Kip and Harley didn't have it in them to continue tonight and this wound would need time before my strength returned. A night here would make our journey safer.

"We'll stay," I told her.

Minerva rewarded me with a dig from another tool, but quickly followed it with a thick paste made of plants that would absorb the toxins and stop the spread through my body.

"Good. That gives you plenty of time to explain why Kip is here," Roane said when the pain stopped making lights burst in front of my eyes.

With both of them staring at me with expectation, there was little chance I would have been able to stay silent even if I wanted to. They were an intense combination.

"You know why I went for her," I said.

"I don't," Minerva interjected.

"The wizards had a prophecy," I explained. "They foretold a woman in the human world who would step into the war and save the Summer Queen."

"Ajeka doesn't need saving," Minerva said bitterly.

"There will come a time when she might, and Kip is the one destined to stand in the way of whatever harm may come to her."

"What harm?" Roane asked. "What exactly was Kip supposed to save her from?"

I shook my head. Minerva finished tending the gash in my leg and we moved back into the living room. The less time the small room was open and the supplies readily visible, the better.

"The wizards didn't tell me that. They told me only that she would save the Summer Queen. They feared that meant if Kip were to fulfill that prophecy, she would secure victory for Ajeka in the war."

"So they sent you to kill her," Minerva said.

There was a hint of disdain in her voice. It was understandable. Many had a contentious relationship with the wizards. Though they were the most trusted and powerful of my advisers, that didn't mean they were always kind and benevolent. In fact, they were a few of the men I would least like to cross. I was never given the full details before my parents died, but I knew enough to know the wizards were instrumental in Minerva's exile.

"It had to be done," I told her. "Once they realized what she would mean to the war, it was obvious she couldn't just be ignored. She had to be stopped before she could fulfill the prophecy. As King of the Blood Court, it was my responsibility to ensure it was done."

"If that's the case, why is she currently in my house getting primped for her debut into the Land of the Sidhe?"

Before I had a chance to answer, Roane's eyes moved over me and to the entrance to the hallway. They widened and his lips parted slightly. I followed his gaze to where Valerie presented her efforts. I knew Harley was there, but I only saw Kip. The front strands of her hair had been calmed into the complex twists and braids favored by the Fae women, while the back hung in the wild, free way that made my heart swell. It tumbled around her shoulders, which were left bare by the low-sweeping fabric of the dress she wore. It was the style of the Fae women, but it had never been as beautiful as it was on her.

"Minerva?" Valerie said. "Supper is ready."

"Come, everyone," Minerva said. "Stryder can tell us more while we eat."

I couldn't keep my eyes off Kip as we sat down on the soft cushions positioned around the low wooden table. Valerie placed platters of food along the length of the table, commenting as she did that it was good she always prepared far more than the two of them needed. Minerva dismissed it as coming from the younger woman's childhood growing up with a seemingly never-ending list of siblings. That might have been true, but it wasn't the only reason she made sure there was plenty of food available. I knew we were not the first travelers to find their way into her home in need of assistance.

When our plates were full and everyone had gotten several bites of the rich, hearty stew into their bellies, I started telling Kip more about the war. Other than Harley, everyone else at the table already knew what I was telling her, but they listened with the same rapt attention. I told her of the brutality of the Summer Queen and her burning drive for total power. It wasn't the first war our land had faced or the first time desire for control had led to the loss of life, but it was the longest and the most intense.

Kip seemed to recoil slightly as I recounted stories of the battlefield. I told her about the people dragged away to serve their lives as slaves to the Summer Court. But she stayed quiet. She listened bravely to everything I had to tell her and didn't try to stop me. When I was finished, she took a long breath.

"And I'm supposed to be the one who saves her?" she asked. "Why would I do that?"

"I don't know," I admitted. "But now you understand the desperation to do anything possible to bring this to an end."

"Even kill someone who had nothing to do with it yet."

"Yes."

"Tell me why you didn't do it. You had every opportunity. And from that story, you had every reason to other than a reluctance to kill somebody who wasn't aware of your war. Why did you change your mind?"

I reached for the carved wooden cup filled with strong berry wine and took a deep sip of it. The taste was unlike anything available in the human world, and it was one of the things that made me homesick while I was away. Now the sweet taste and comforting, steeling warmth as it moved down my throat and through my chest gave me a minute to think. I wanted to give her as much information as I could, but this wasn't the time to tell her she was my fated mate. Not here. Not with everyone else at the table.

"Like you said, you haven't done anything yet. You didn't even know who I was or who any of the other Fae men were. I knew what the wizards told me, but it was so hard to see you as a threat. Beyond that, I changed my mind because I saw another way to protect my people."

"What do you mean?" Roane asked.

"Even if we don't understand why Kip is important or what her role will be, she's obviously a powerful force. If instead of obliterating that force, we could instead take it on to our own side and use it for ourselves, we could bring an end to this bloodshed."

"How?" Kip asked.

"If you have the power to protect the Summer Queen, then you have the power to end her."

"We've come this far," she said. "For now, I might as well keep going with you."

I nodded.

"We are a far distance from the Blood Court. I have to warn you it will be a long and difficult journey. The clothes the women have given you will help you to blend at a glance, but it won't fool any Fae for long. We will travel through dangerous lands and across battlefields to get to the court. You have to be ready to face what comes."

4

Kip

"Do you think they're going to be safe sleeping out there?" I looked over at Harley. She was busy getting herself ready, fluffing pillows and shaking out blankets on one of the two beds that barely fit into Valerie's room.

"Stryder and Roane?" she suddenly stopped to look up at me.

"Yeah. We're in here, nice and comfy, while they're outside. You heard what Stryder said. We're far away from his court and it's dangerous out here. He already nearly died because of the poison on that goblin's knife. I think that warrants a real place to sleep."

Harley studied me curiously. "Minerva said the procedure she did on him took effect and he is out of danger. You know this isn't the first time he's been injured in a battle. Besides, it's not like they rolled out their sleeping bags in the front yard. They're sleeping in the lean-to behind the house. They're fine, in fact, they probably like it."

I huffed. "I'm sure. I just wish that they'd let them sleep inside."

She rolled her eyes. "It's not like Stryder gave them a lot of choice," Harley pointed out. She deepened her voice, mimicking Stryder. "'We're sleeping outside,'" she walked around the room, her chest puffed out. "I'm a manly man, nobody tells me what to do. I kill bad guys for breakfast and wisk women away on my steed." She eyed me. "Well, maybe only one woman in particular."

I threw a pillow at her, trying not to smile. "Shut up. You're ridiculous."

She grinned. "Not as ridiculous as you'd like to think."

I ignored that comment. "Just because he's manly," manly," and incredibly sexy, I added in my head,, I added in my head, "doesn't mean it's any less dangerous."

"Stryder insisting on doing things that seem unduly complicated and dangerous is also par for the course." She frowned. "Maybe I should be more worried."

I got into my own bed and rolled on my side to look at her. "If I didn't know any better, I'd think you were starting to get a soft spot in that steel-encased heart of yours for a certain man of the Fae persuasion."

She crawled into her bed. "That's going a little bit too far. I realize he is a touch on the touchy side when it comes to me, but it's all just too much. I mean, with all his chivalrousness and the way he's constantly trying to make sure I'm all right, it's like he thinks I'm completely incompetent or something. That might work for some women, I guess, but if Roane thinks he's going to sweep me off my feet, he's in for some serious disappointment."

She was so intent on staring up at the ceiling that she didn't see the smile that crossed my face. "I was actually talking about Stryder, but that was pretty telling."

Her eyes snapped over to me. She narrowed them and I held up my hands innocently. The spark between the two of them was obvious, but so was Harley's adamant resistance to it. She was going to fight any sort of feelings as hard as she could. That was something about her that hadn't changed since we were children. The walls she put up then were to protect her from the unpredictability and turmoil that came from being in the foster care system and the family she wanted so much but that never came. They stayed in place as an adult so she never had to deal with those feelings again.

"I am pretty impressed by you, though," she said, looking over at me with a smile.

"Why would you be impressed by me?" I asked. "Because of my exceptional ability to only get attention from men who want to kill me, kidnap me, or both?"

She laughed and propped herself up on her elbow to look at me better.

"Well, yeah. That is a rare and exceptional talent. But what I really mean is how important you are. The future of an entire war hinges on you. That's pretty incredible."

I sighed and rolled over onto my back. "Yeah. Who would have thought I'd hit adulthood and be off saving the world?" I'd meant it sarcastically, but Harley didn't take it that way.

"I did," she said. I looked over at her and she shrugged. "Even when we were little girls, I knew you were going to grow up to be somebody. Really somebody. You were always able to handle everything so well. Everybody liked you. That's why it didn't surprise me when you were the one who got adopted."

A sharp pain stabbed through my heart. It did every time we talked about that one unchangeable, painful division between us. No matter how close Harley and I were, no matter how devoted we were to our friendship or committed to always sticking together, it was there. A family had chosen me. No one chose her.

"You know how much it always hurt me that you aren't adopted," I told her. "You deserved a family."

"You are my family, Kip. We're in this together, no matter what, just like we always have been." Her grin got wider, and a flash of mischief glittered in her eyes. "Besides, I was always the one who was up for an adventure."

I laughed.

"Yes, you were. Every time we had to change houses or deal with horrible foster siblings, you were able to make some game out of it. It was so much less scary when you said we were just on an adventure or facing some mythical challenge to reach the next level. I never knew if you were going to pretend we were pirates or gladiators or in some video game, but it worked. You made it feel like something to be excited about and that made it less scary."

"It's the same thing now," she said. "All this is one big adventure. Think about it, Kip. We are in a world we didn't even know existed, surrounded by a species we never would have believed were real. And we get to see it all. Not only that, but you get to save it."

"Or destroy it. You know. Choices. We'll see how I feel when the time comes."

She laughed, then fell quiet as she headed toward sleep. I lay awake for a while longer, thinking about what she said. I'd come here for Mac, to make his death mean something, but now it felt like more.

When we woke up the next morning, there were carefully folded packs of clothing at the foot of our beds. Harley and I changed into long gowns much like the ones Minerva and Valerie were wearing the night before. We did our best to reconstruct the braids that had loosened and disheveled in sleep. We added our nightgowns into the packs of clothes and walked out into the rest of the house toward the smell of breakfast being made.

Despite all reassurances from Harley the night before, I was relieved to see Stryder and Roane already in the front room. Stryder's eyes traced along the emerald green dress I'd chosen and his gaze met mine own. A shiver rolled over me at his heated look. His wings were tucked on either side of him, but not bound. The sight of them made my belly tighten. I was intrigued and enraptured with them. I was even more attracted to him when he was in this more natural form. It was like I was seeing something special, a secret he only shared with select people.

I settled onto one of the cushions at the side of the table, trying not to gaze his way too much, and Valerie set a mug in front of me. The smell coming up from it was similar to coffee, but stronger and with a sweet undercurrent like dark chocolate and cherries. I took a sip of it and felt the jolt go through to my fingertips.

Stryder laughed at the expression on my face as I set the mug back down on the table. "It's a little more powerful than what you are used to," he said. "But get as much of it as you can in. You'll need the energy for the trip."

The men finished eating first and went outside to call the horses. By the time Harley and I had eaten and gathered our packs, Ominous Thunder and Aramis had been loaded with the rest of our supplies.

"Be careful," Minerva said, her arms across her chest in a nervous gesture.

"We will be. You too. They might come by," he answered her.

He didn't specify who but the older woman's lips tightened into a thin line and she gave a sharp nod. She knew who he was talking about.

His eyes moved to me again, and I held his gaze, unable to look away. Holding out his hand, I clasped it and he lifted me easily onto the horse. He seemed much better than he was last night and relief moved through me. If the poison had really taken hold, he wouldn't have had the chance to wake up this morning, much less be putting me on a horse. But actually feeling the power of his muscles and the security of his arms gave me far more confidence and reassurance than just being told everything was going to work out. He settled in in front of me and his warm body against mine was comforting.

Valerie reached up to hand Stryder his sword, and he slipped it into its sheath, then glanced over at Roane to make sure he and Harley were ready on Aramis. The men nodded at each other and with a final goodbye, we headed back into the forest. Our pace was slower this time and I found myself enjoying the rhythmic motion of the animal beneath me.

"So...Ominous Thunder," I said.

"Yes."

"Did he come with that name?"

"No."

"So you chose that name for him on purpose?" I asked.

"Yes. His hooves sound like thunder. I'd like to think it's a warning to my enemies. The kind of sound to inspire fear in people who hear it."

I laughed. "Just be prepared that I am absolutely going to be making fun of you for that sometime when things aren't as stabby and chase-y."

He glanced back at me, smiling. "I'll brace myself."

The sight of his grin made my stomach flutter. I settled into the rhythm of the horse and let out a sigh. "Will I get my own horse sometime?"

"I'm sure you will," Stryder said.

"How about my own sword?"

"Maybe."

"Stryder?" I rested my head on his back, my arms tight around his muscled waist.

"Yes, Kip?"

"Will you teach me how to ride a horse and use a sword?"

He chuckled and pat my hands, then rested his there, causing another flight of butterflies to lurch straight from my stomach to my chest. "Don't worry. You'll learn."

5

Stryder

I had spent my life with the world at my feet and able to do virtually anything I wanted, when I wanted. Not anymore. Having Kip so close to me, her warm, soft body snuggled up against my back, was torture. I wanted to reach around and touch her, to reassure her, to kiss her. To pull her into my lap, strip her of the beautiful emerald gown that brought out the fire in her hair, and run my fingers over every inch of her perfectly delicate skin. To have her writhing under me, begging for more of everything I could give her.

Just the mere thought had me gripping my reins tighter. I was glad I'd positioned her behind me because my dick was rock hard; holding all these emotions inside me was complete and utter agony. Keeping my intensifying feelings for her hidden was harder than I ever could have imagined. She was in every thought that went through my head, during every breath I took. Knowing she was meant to belong to me gave me strength and determination far beyond what I already had, but also made me feel out of control and anxious. I wanted to bury myself in her, get lost in her touch. But I couldn't.

First, she had no idea what we were to each other. Not yet anyways. Secondly, I had to do everything I could to focus on what was ahead of us. There were other challenges besides just the Summer Queen.

When we'd fought the queen back, I would figure everything else out.

The morning burned away into midday and then into the afternoon. We'd taken sips from the canteens hanging at the sides of the horses and eaten pieces of dried meat and bread from sacks I had hung so they were easily accessible on the trail, but Kip and Harley were getting uncomfortable. I could feel Kip wriggling and shifting her weight behind me and occasionally she would grumble or let out a deep sigh. I knew eventually we would have to stop for a break, but I didn't want to lose time. I wanted to travel faster. According to Roane, we were desperately needed back in the Blood Court, but I was also trying to be understanding to the women. Plus, traveling without thought through the land was unwise. Danger lurked everywhere.

Finally, the dark thicket of woods let up and we walked out into a sun-dappled clearing edged with a crystal blue creek.

"We'll stop here for a bit," I said, slowing Thunder.

"Are you sure? My ass still has a tiny bit of feeling in it. A little further and we could achieve total numbness," Kip muttered.

It was gentler than the string of complaints dotted with colorful profanities Harley offered, but the sentiment was the same. I got down off the horse and reached up to help Kip down. She slipped as she tried to move one stiff leg, but I caught her. Our eyes met as her body pressed against mine and I heard her breath catch in her throat. I could have put her down faster, but I didn't want the connection to stop. Easing her down slowly, I let her body slide along mine until she was on her feet in front of me. Her hands stayed resting on my shoulders, her eyes not moving from mine as her mouth opened slightly and the tip of her tongue ran along the pink swell of her bottom lip.

Heat ran through my body and into my blood and I begged the gods that she couldn't tell how aroused I was feeling. I could feel her presence through every inch of me and the desire for her intensified. I never wanted to stop touching her, to stop feeling her skin against mine and her breath along my neck.

But all too soon, Kip's eyes moved away from mine and she took a step back from me. Her hands ran along her arms like she could feel the same tingling along her skin that I could when we touched. The look in her eyes was uncertain, and I knew there were still so many questions going through her mind. She was struggling with trusting me, and I couldn't blame her. All that mattered was that she was here. She had come along with me and was willing to face what was ahead.

"I am seriously second-guessing my willingness to go along with this," Harley said as she walked back and forth a few feet away. "No one told me the traveling part was going to suck this much."

"You'll get used to it," Roane said encouragingly.

"You don't really have a choice," I told her. "This is how we travel here. You're not going to find a comfortable air-conditioned compact to snatch along the trail."

She gave me a nasty glare and turned her back to me, stretching from side to side to try to loosen up the tightness that comes from hours on the back of a horse. The women weren't accustomed to spending as much time traveling like this, but they were going to have to get used to it as fast as possible.

"I didn't snatch anything," Harley said. "I *borrowed*. Besides, if riding around on horses is the only way you would travel in this place, how did you know so much about cars?"

"That wasn't the first time I've been to the human world," I told her.

She looked over at Roane hopefully. "He's kidding, right?

Riding horses isn't really the only way you travel. There's going to be something else?"

"It's not the only way," Roane told her. "There are boats in some places and in the courts there are carriages. They are drawn by horses, but also there are the Dragons."

He said it with a casual shrug, like that was just something the women should expect. Her eyes slid over to him and she let out a laugh. When he didn't laugh with her, the smile drooped. "Oh, you're serious."

Roane nodded.

Kip gasped and Harley swallowed hard. Their eyes were wide and I knew both were envisioning massive scaly creatures swooping out of the sky and picking them up for an afternoon snack. Now would be the time to redirect their focus.

"We're not going to be here for long," I announced. "Enough time to eat, get a drink, and stretch your muscles. Then we need to keep moving."

"Dragons?" Kip asked.

Apparently my technique didn't work.

"You don't need to worry about that," I told her. "They are not very common and most are isolated to very specific areas of the Land. Only a few actually use them for transportation."

"Comforting," she said, unconvinced.

I unloaded a bag of food from Thunder's side and laid it out on the ground for everyone to take from. Roane flopped himself down into the grass to take a break, but I stayed on my feet. Sitting down would draw out my energy and I needed to be as alert as possible.

"What's next?" he asked.

"We have a meeting," I told him.

"A meeting?" Kip asked. "What do you mean?"

"Some of my advisors are waiting for me."

"The wizards?"

"No. They are still in the Blood Court and I will deal with

them later. These are some of the trusted men in my army. I need them to know what's going on so we can plan how to move forward."

"They don't know I'm here, do they?" she asked.

"Not yet. It would be better for me to explain it to them when I see them. We don't want to keep them waiting. If you're finished eating, splash some cold water on your face and let's get going."

"It's not my face that's bothering me," Harley pointed out. "But I don't think going and sitting in the creek over there is going to refresh my ass in quite the same way."

"I'll put an extra blanket on Aramis's back," Roane told her. "It will make it more comfortable for you."

Kip and I glanced at each other, but her eyes fell away quickly.

WE TRAVELED for several more hours and the sun was beginning to set by the time we reached the meeting place. I climbed down from his back and lead Thunder to the small cave at the base of a hill.

"Benson," I called out.

A face appeared at the mouth of the cave, then two men emerged. "Stryder, you found us," he said earnestly, his eyes moving to the two women. "What's going on?"

"I need to speak with you," I told him.

He nodded and the two walked back into the cave. Roane and I secured our horses so they wouldn't wander far and followed my advisors into the shadows of the cavern. It was dark and cold for the first several yards, then we stepped out into a chamber lit by candlelight. Four men sat on the stone floor around a fire one had enchanted to release no smoke.

"Men," I said. "Thank you for coming to meet with me on such short notice."

Before I left for the human world, the men and I had agreed to meet back here when I returned. The night we stayed at Minerva's house, I used an enchantment the Wizards had created for us to alert them of my return so they would know it was time to come back together.

"We are glad to see you have returned," Silas said. "But it looks like we won't be receiving news that you were successful in your mission."

He was choosing his words carefully. These men knew why I went to the human world and what I was supposed to do there. They were thoughtful in their discretion, not wanting to create trouble where there wasn't any or leak any secrets if untrusted ears were nearby.

"Things have changed," I told them. "I need you to listen. There's no time to be wasted."

We sat down with them and I explained the situation as briefly but clearly as I could. My words skimmed past the detail of Kip being my fated mate. I didn't plan on telling them that. The opposition would be too great to deal with right now.

When I finished, Benson, the oldest of the group, looked at each of the others and then nodded. "You've done what you believed was right, King. We have no power to argue against you. But be warned. The deaths of the Summer Queen's servants in the human world didn't go unnoticed, and neither has the disappearance of the woman they were sent to bring back. They're coming for you. You will be targeted by all of the Queen's forces and her many allies."

"I'm already targeted," I said. "They have been coming for me since before the war began."

"It's different now. They are gaining traction and pushing deeper into the Blood Court. And with Kip here..." Benson's voice trailed off as if he couldn't bring himself to say what went through his mind. "They will stop at nothing to prevent her from being used by the Blood Court and our allies."

I drew in a deep breath to force back the tightness in my chest, refusing to let my face betray any hesitation or emotion. This was going to be even more difficult than I had imagined.

6

K*ip* Stryder didn't let us rest for long in the cavern with his advisors. The warmth of the fire and the hypnotic dancing of the flames was enough to lull me and I lay down on a tightly woven blanket while he continued to talk to the men. I didn't fully understand everything they were saying. It was complex military strategy interwoven with code and references to people and places completely unfamiliar to me. I drifted to sleep to them discussing the front line and how to best defend the Court.

What felt like far too soon, he roused me from my slumber and brought us all back out into the woods. The darkness was deep and inky, telling me I had only gotten a few hours of rest at the very most. I didn't know if Stryder had slept at all, but he was just as determined as we climbed onto Thunder's back and continued on.

Spending so many long hours on the back of the animal was so uncomfortable, I was sure there was no way I'd be able to relax. I was surprised when the sudden shifting of Stryder's body startled me awake and I realized I had rested my head on his back and drifted off again. Sunlight was coming up through the branches of the trees and ahead of us the tight spacing of the trunks thinned and dissipated until in the distance I could see a lit, open space.

It wasn't a vibrant, piercing brightness like the glare of the sunlight when we were first traveling and before we sank into the dark shadows of the woods. Instead, it was an almost opalescent glow that drew me toward it. Stryder moved to get down off the horse and when he noticed I was looking at him, he offered me a smile.

"We can take a break here," he said. "It's safer. Although be on your guard. Just because something is lovely doesn't mean it can be trusted. People learn that here."

The cryptic words hung between us and I looked into his eyes. "I've already learned that," I told him and a guilty look flashed on his face. When he didn't answer, I looked around. "Where are we?"

We were approaching the beautiful glow and I saw lush rolling hills and more delicate trees dotted across the land in front of us. The creek we had long since put behind us had reappeared and wound through the intensely green grass. Stryder reached out for me and helped me down so I could walk alongside him.

"These," he said as we stepped beyond the woods and into the glow, "are the Mist Realms."

I gasped at the sound of the name. This was what Mac had told me about on my twenty-first birthday. All around me some of the words he had spoken of came to life. It was like he was there, crafting them as I walked into the beautiful space. Something cool touched my face. At first, I thought it was water, then I remembered him describing the tiny creatures who lived in this realm.

I held out my hand and watched as several minuscule blue and shimmering pale beings settled into my palm. Holding it up closer to my face, I looked at them. From this vantage point I could see long, slender bodies and angular, pointed wings. Wide eyes stared back at me and almost as quickly as they had landed, they flitted away.

"This is incredible," I whispered.

"We'll be able to walk here for a while, give you a rest from the horses," Stryder told me. "We'll have to keep moving, though."

I noted the dark circles under his eyes, the stiff way he held himself. "You need to rest."

He frowned. "I have to keep watch. The Summer Army could come at any time and if I'm not vigilant, they could wipe us out before we even know they are here."

"If you don't sleep, you're going to destroy yourself before you can do any good." Worry for his safety and health compounded with frustration at his stubbornness made me feel on edge. "Did you sleep at all when we are at Minerva and Valerie's house?"

His eyes narrowed. "I don't need sleep like you humans do."

"I disagree." I crossed my arms across my chest, digging in.

"And I didn't ask for your opinion." He took a step forward into my personal space, scowling. "My duty is to protect you and your friend. I'm even responsible for Roane. I cannot afford to let my guard down."

"Which is exactly what you're doing by not resting. Everyone knows that in the human world." I couldn't help but notice how tall he was, towering over me, his firm and muscled chest so close to my face. I wanted to lean into his arms, take comfort in his closeness. But my own annoyance at his lack of self care kept me from it. That, and the fact that it would be incredibly awkward for the both of us.

"We're not in the human world."

"Don't I know it," I said, blinking up at him.

"Why can't you see I'm just trying to keep you safe?" His throat bobbed.

"And why can't *you* see you're running yourself into the ground and are going to put all of us at even more risk because of your stubbornness?"

"I'm not being stubborn," he said through gritted teeth.

"Oh, really? Fooled the hell out of me because right now all I'm hearing is a temper-tantrum in the making."

"I'm not having a temper-tantrum." He grabbed my wrist, pulling me closer and shooting tingles up my arm and into my chest. "I'll let you in on something – this is war. That means being constantly on alert, even if you're exhausted."

"And I'll let you in on something," I whispered then leaned closer. An electric current buzzed between us as my lips hovered near his ear. "I've heard that word enough fucking times to be pretty well set for the rest of my life. It's really losing its pizazz at this point."

"I don't even know what pizazz means, but I assure you, it has nothing to do with the reality of what we're going through," he retorted. "And don't talk to me about fucking or I'll certainly have to show you exactly how well I know what that word means."

Eyes widening, I stumbled back, his hold on my wrist keeping me from going too far. My throat suddenly felt dry and my whole body heated. I pulled at the top of my dress, wishing I was back in my comfortable clothes. I swallowed hard, trying to get some moisture back into my mouth. He didn't move back, or even look ashamed of his words but kept his gaze, intense and fierce, on my face.

Tension between us buzzed, making the air heavy. There was mere inches between us. I suddenly felt very vulnerable before him, with the image of him showing me exactly what he meant flashing through my mind. I narrowed my eyes on his lips, flicking my tongue out to trace my dry lips. I wanted to take that last step forward and touch him. Know what it felt like to caress the firm notch of his clavicle, the hard lines of his jaw. Press my lips against the softness of his throat, his lips, find out if they were supple or firm or both. I finally opened my mouth, stuttering, trying to ignore what he'd just said because I didn't know how else to respond.

"The truth is, I'm starving, my entire body feels like it has become a permanent fixture of the back of your horse, and I don't appreciate having my safety in the hands of someone who is going to slip into sleep-deprived delusions any second. I don't know this place. If you fell asleep, I wouldn't be able to navigate through it while dragging your sleeping ass behind the horse."

He huffed. "Thank you for the courtesy of not even letting me sleep on my own horse."

"If I'm going to be traipsing through a place I have never seen, and could start discovering messed up things like those Bogles at any second, I'm going to need all the space on the horse I can get."

He suddenly burst into laughter, the low, sexy rumble of it rolling over my skin. I grinned, breaking free from my irritation, totally entranced by the sound of it. I suddenly wanted to remember all the jokes I'd ever heard in my lifetime just to hear the sound of it again.

"Fine," he said, his hand landing on my hip to urge me forward. "We'll stay longer next time we stop. We will be safer in the Mists. They likely wouldn't look for us in this part of the land."

"What are you thinking about?" Stryder asked a while later as we continued to walk slowly through the realm. I didn't know where we were going or when we would stop, but being on my feet rather than on the back of the horse was a welcome reprieve and I was willing it to continue on that way.

"Mac," I shrugged. "The bookshop."

It wasn't completely true. I was thinking about my dear friend, but I also couldn't stop my mind from drifting back to Stryder's wings. He hadn't bound them again and they hung powerful and impressive down his back. I wanted to touch them, but Harley and Roane so close behind us stopped me. I couldn't explain why, but that was a moment I didn't want to share with them.

"What about it?"

"I miss him. It hurts so much more than I ever would have thought. Not that I ever would have thought it would be easy for him to die. I guess I just tried to pretend something like that would never happen to me again. Not after my parents. But now it's like him dying, especially after everything I know about him now, brought back all the pain of losing them, too. It's still so hard to believe that he's actually gone. I can't wrap my head around the idea that when I go back to Glendale, he's not going to be there. I'll walk into the bookshop and he's not going to be teetering on the top of a ladder somewhere trying to clean off the books or organizing shelves of volumes people haven't touched in years. I won't get to hear him be so excited about the new stash he has or give me the rundown of everything customers bought when I wasn't there. It's just not going to be the same. He was so kind and sweet. Eccentric, but wonderful. I wish I had gotten the chance to know him better."

"I'm sorry. I understand what it's like to lose someone important to you. But why were you thinking about the bookshop?"

"Without him there, it won't open again. Not until I'm back. I'll take over it for him and run it the way I know he would want me to. It's hard to think about it sitting there empty and alone. I might not have had the chance to get to know him in the way that I could have, but I want to find out as much about him, and how he knew so much, as possible before I go home."

Stryder's eyes burned into me, but I couldn't decipher the emotion in them. He didn't say anything else about Mac or the bookshop but pointed ahead of us to what looked like a row of tents draped in the trees.

"That's where we'll stop," he told me.

We were nearly to the shelters when his words came back into my mind. "Why did you say simply because something is lovely it doesn't mean it could be trusted? Are we actually safe here?"

"We are safe," he said. "It's just important to always be aware of what's around you. Of yourself. Remember they aren't the same."

He turned away from me and I felt a sinking feeling in my stomach, but the soft touch of the tiny creatures on my cheek and a breeze that ruffled through my hair released the tightness and the dark thoughts drifted away.

7

Stryder

I didn't really know how exhausted I was until I stepped into the shade of the tent. All of the bags and supplies had been taken off the horses and Thunder and Aramis were roaming happily through the cool, softly glowing land. Without the sun beating down on them and the heavy packs on their backs, they could relax. The gentle touch of the sprites cooled their skin and relaxed their muscles. They would be happy here. It would be hard to convince them to continue on when the time came to move out of the realm.

Now that the work had been done, I could tell myself it was time to rest. As soon as I did, the happiness and fatigue pushed down on my shoulders and I dropped down onto one of the hammocks strung up beneath the drape of the tent. I didn't even have the energy to take off my boots or remove my sword from its sheath.

"Is he going to be all right?" Kip's voice asked some time later.

My eyelids fluttered but I couldn't lift them all the way. I felt her beside me, felt the touch of her hand resting on my arm.

"He'll be fine," a musical voice said. It was one of the Mist Nymphs, another inhabitant of the realm. "He just needs to rest."

Larger than the sprites that swarmed through the air and felt like a sprinkle of rain or a fine brush of water from a stream, the Mist Nymphs were usually shy and hesitant near outsiders. But they knew me well and had apparently accepted Kip, and likely Harley, as an extension of me.

I felt Kip move down and the weight of my sword leave my sheath. A few seconds later, she untied my boots and pulled them from my hot, aching feet. The relief made me sink back into deep sleep again. I didn't know how long I was asleep before the voices came through to me again.

"Here. Take this. It will help him," another Mist Nymph said.

Kip made an acknowledging sound and then something cold and sweet ran over my lips and rushed into my mouth. The taste was intoxicating and as soon as I swallowed, my body felt stronger. After a few more seconds, I opened my eyes. Kip pulled the piece of pink and purple fruit away from my mouth and looked down at me.

"You don't have to wake up," she said. "Get some more sleep."

"Eat more first," a Mist Nymph I knew as Gael insisted, stepping up to Kip's side and lifting her hand to bring the fruit to my mouth again.

I knew the taste of the delicate, sweet flesh, but hadn't had any of it in many years. This was a precious, extraordinarily rare fruit that only grew in the Mist Realms. The restorative properties could give a person almost insurmountable strength for a time and bring them back from the brink of death. Some suggested from death itself.

"I didn't know any more of this existed," I told Gael. "So many have said they came here to find it, but there was none to be had."

"None for them, perhaps," she told me. "We've been hiding it to keep it from the Summer Fae."

I smiled at her and took the fruit in my hands, squeezing as much of the juice into my mouth as I could get from it.

"Thank you," I said.

"Rest now. That piece will give you your strength back." She smiled at us and left the tent.

"How long have I been sleeping?" I asked.

"Most of the day," Kip told me. "It's almost time for the rest of us to go to bed."

I nodded and let my eyes close again.

The combination of the effects of the fruit and the sound of movements woke me again some time later. All the rest of the light was gone and there was only the glow of stars beyond the tent. I saw a figure and realized Kip was leaving. I got out of the hammock and followed after her. She was walking away from the shelters alone and I quickly caught up with her.

"Kip," I called out quietly so I wouldn't disturb anyone else.

She turned around sharply but went back to her walk when she saw it was me, slowing down to let me meet her. "Are you feeling better?"

"You can't come out here alone," I told her.

"Actually, it seems I can," she said, a mysterious smile on her face. "See?" She did a little twirl as if to indicate to me that she was in fact out alone. "Here I am."

"You know what I mean," I said with a bit more force than I had intended. "You can't wander away by yourself. It isn't safe."

Her eyes narrowed and she planted her hands on her hips. "That's funny coming from someone who not too long ago was trying to *kill* me."

"Things have changed," I argued. "You know that."

"We'll see," she said. "Besides, you said we were safe here."

"I also said you needed to be careful."

"I couldn't sleep, and I couldn't just lie there." She scowled, ignoring me to continue down the path. "I just need to wander a little bit, to think about things for a bit."

She obviously had a lot on her mind, and I fell into step beside her, letting her walk silently for a while. All around us, the Mist Realm bloomed into its nightly beauty. This area was breathtaking at night, one of my favorite sights outside of my own home. Kip looked around, taking it all in, and occasionally letting out a sigh as she absorbed the new sights, the musical soft sounds, and the sweet delicate smells of the Mist Realm.

Wanting to share everything with her, I held out my hand. "Come here, I want to show you something."

She looked at my hand, uncertainty on her face. "I'm not sure I like surprises anymore."

"You'll like this one." I took her hand, not waiting for her to accept it, and a shock of desire coursed through me. Tension sizzled in the air between us. I knew she felt the same thing, could hear it in her breath as it trembled out in a long exhale. My mind wandered back to the kiss in the parking lot, the tension between us only hours ago as we'd argued. Stubborn, frustrating woman. I'd wanted to take her in my arms, throw her over my shoulder and steal her away from the world.

I led her beyond the area to a lake that spread out from the base of large rocks like a sheet of glass. Through the serene, clear surface of the water we could watch bioluminescent fish swish and dance with each other in swirls of pastel blues, pinks, and purples. Her eyes brightened as soon as she saw them, her face displaying her wonder at the sight. "I've changed my mind. I like surprises again."

I grinned, and she sat at the edge, leaning over to watch them intently. The colors shimmering over the surface highlighted her beauty, exquisite and ethereal. Unable to keep myself from being far from her, I sat next to her, my side brushing hers and she shivered with the contact. After a long stretch of silence, she turned to me abruptly. "Why did you save me?"

I swallowed hard, looking away. "I already explained that to you."

"I know what you said, but I don't think that's the whole story."

My heart squeezed and my stomach turned as I felt like I was being torn apart. I debated with myself, struggling to decide what to tell her. I knew eventually she would have to know, but there was only so much she could handle right now.

"There's just something special about you and it stopped me," I said abruptly.

Kip recoiled slightly at the gruffness of my response.

"That's it?" she asked. "You're going to pull the 'you're special' card and I'm supposed to just accept it?"

"It's all I have to offer you right now."

"Why?" she asked, obviously dissatisfied by the answer I was giving her.

"Because right now we need to concentrate on the work at hand and getting to the Blood Court as soon as we can. My forces will only be able to hold off the Summer Court for so long and with what Roane has told me, the time is getting short." I stood up and looked down at her. "Come on. You need to sleep while you can. We leave at first light."

I reached down for her hand and helped her up. She stood so our bodies were only inches apart and I could hear her breath catch in her throat. My fingertips tingled with the need to touch her. My mouth watered at the sweep of her tongue across her lips and the slight tilt of her face toward mine like she was seeking a kiss. I wanted to oblige her and satisfy my own need, but the touch of her lips would be too much for me in that moment. Instead, I walked away, gritting my teeth and fighting against everything inside me with every step. Behind me, I could hear Kip let out a frustrated sigh.

8

Stryder

After hours of traveling the next day, darkness began to overtake us as the trees thickened above and suffocated the light and oxygen, leaving a musty, wet dim light that drained the lungs and made us squint our eyes. I knew this path, but it had been a long time since I had traveled it, since before The War in fact. It was dangerous then for those who weren't careful, but now it had a sense of foreboding that could not be ignored.

"It was so pretty before," Kip said, almost to herself. "What is this place?"

"We are out of the Mist Realms. I've been here before, but it was long ago," I said.

I hesitated to say more because I didn't want to scare her or Harley, but I knew the dangers of this place. And what lived here.

We walked silently for a while, stepping over roots and boulders that had made their way into the path, as the trees seemed to creep slowly toward us. Soon we were surrounded by thick brush and the path ahead of us was hidden behind large branches of thick leaves. I pushed one aside and felt my foot sink. Grabbing hold of the branch, I yelled out to the group behind me.

"Everyone stop moving," I shouted. "Quicksand! Roane, help me out."

Roane reached out an arm and I took it, pulling to swing myself off the branch toward him. I landed just inches from where the ground turned to a sandy trap. Looking just to the left, I could see the path had forked, and a way around the sand wound through thick woods.

"We have to take the other way. Be careful. These are the Elder Trees."

"What are the Elder Trees?"

"Demons. Or so the legend says," Roane said.

I began walking toward the other path, unsheathing my sword to cut down some of the branches blocking our way. "Long ago, when the Fae were still taming this land for our needs, there were demons of the woods. Our magic was weak in those days, but as it grew, we used it to fight the forces of the demons. Spells were cast that set them rooted to the ground, and trees to grow around them. It is said that the demons inside them still live, and will move their branches to create false paths, making travelers lose their way. When they are alone and lost and weak, the demons are said to feed on them."

"How? I mean, they are just trees, right?"

"It's just a legend. Even still the Elder Trees are known for being hallmarks of a land where paths can be confusing. We must be careful and stay together, no matter what."

I hacked through the branches and we moved on in silence again, the oppression of the forest closing in around us. After a while I could see more light and knew a clearing was ahead of us. The women looked tired and our horses needed rest. It was time to stop and the clearing would be ideal. So close to the Elder Trees, it wouldn't be a place many would brave to venture. But I knew my way around the woods and had encountered the demons several times before. They had no sway over me. I increased my speed and pushed through to just a few feet from the exit of the woods when I stopped cold.

A sound rippled through the air like a horn. Behind me I heard Roane shush the women and the horses, and I turned to him. Our eyes met and I could sense something in them that I rarely saw. Fear.

I nodded to him and he handed the reins to Harley, stepping up beside me as we both crouched down low. I held my hand up to signal Kip and Harley to stay back, but Kip joined us anyway. Ugh. This woman. She took direction so well.

"What was that?" she asked in a too-loud whisper.

"Pigs," Roane said.

"Pigs? I didn't even know you had things like that here. What the hell are we scared of pigs for?"

"War Pigs," Roane expanded, turning his attention to the clearing, peering to see if he could find any trace of them.

Time was slipping away. If the horn had sounded, it meant they had found something to hunt. Likely us.

"Excuse me...what?" Kip asked. "Are we talking somebody strapped a sword onto Wilbur and sent him after us?"

"Not exactly. War Pigs are a name we have given them," I said. "They are hybrid creatures, created specifically for battle. They have no loyalty but to the one who pays the highest price. Out here though, these live on their own. Their loyalty is to themselves."

"Pigs are an abomination," Roane added. "They are not meant for this or any other world. And they know it. They destroy everything in their path and seek things out to destroy--anything and everything near them. They're bred for war. They fight well, and they fight viciously."

Roane was about to say something else when a spear passed inches from his face, burying itself into a tree behind us. Kip scrambled backward as a creature crashed through the woods ahead of us. The body was only four feet tall, but the menace it produced might as well have been from a giant. Its fat, hairy body was wet with sweat, and it stood on hooves that were covered in dirt and dried blood. It was thick and fast and had a snout with nostrils the size of a fist from which snot flew out with every deep, heaving breath. Its eyes were low and wide, taking in a panoramic view of what surrounded it, making it harder to sneak up on them. Thick, broad shoulders were connected to short, lean arms, one of which held a knife. It was ugly and terrifying and damned fast.

The War Pig.

I jumped into its path, grabbing at the handle of the knife and trying to wrench it away. It struggled with me a moment before biting down into my shoulder, its two rows of sharpened teeth digging into me and sending streams of blood down my back. I yelled in pain as Roane circled behind it, but the creature saw him coming. It released me and tackled Roane low, sending him backwards into a wide tree stump. Somewhere I could hear Harley yell out and I assumed it was in surprise and fear for Roane.

"Kip! They have Kip," she screamed.

I turned to look at her and then the direction she pointed. A War Pig had her by the waist and was dragging her toward the clearing. I took off toward her at a sprint, pushing heavy limbs out of my way with one hand as I drew my sword with the other. Roane, was struggling with his own pig, who'd stuck him a few times with the blade but Roane was a fighter, and could find a way out of this. Kip had no idea what she was up against.

Suddenly I was out of the wooded area and into the clearing, the War Pig with Kip ahead of me. It was heading for a large Elder Tree in the center of the clearing, and what looked like an altar before it. I knew what that meant, and my need to protect her sent a bone-rattling surge of adrenaline through me. Two steps farther and I unfurled my wings and took to the sky.

The water in the air provided more resistance, slowing me down, but it was still faster than running. I had almost caught up to them when I saw it slam her onto the altar, her body limp. I tried to convince myself that she was only unconscious, but fear and anger coursed through me at the mere thought of her being seriously hurt. I dove down, my sword out like I was an arrow from the heavens.

At the last second, the War Pig jumped out of the way, and I landed hard on the ground. A thick, muscular leg kicked me in the ribs and I rolled away from it. Forcing myself to my knees, I looked up and saw Kip's eyes opening, looking toward me, as above her, the War Pig unsheathed a knife. It raised it up as I leapt to my feet, tearing after it.

"She's mine," I screamed as I dove over her, the blade slashing into my wing, piercing my back as I lay on top of her. "You can't take what was made for me."

Yanking myself up, I met the pig's eyes, wild with hatred and hunger. Drawing another knife, he tried to slash at me. A guttural scream came from deep within my chest as I drew my hand forward, my own magic building from the center of my chest. A white-hot fire like bile in the back of my throat consumed me until I could feel it coming from my every pore, seeping out onto my skin, where it collected like sweat, and then streamed to my fingers.

I clapped my hands together, magic shooting from my fingers, exploding the world around me in light and fire and blood. My roar mixed with the high-pitched sound of raw magic being summoned from the world around me, and the ground shook beneath my feet. Trees at the edge of the woods withered and the grass around the altar turned brown and died instantly. The remnants of the pig showered down around me, the magic having exploded it from the inside.

I fell, collapsing off the altar and onto the ground, realization running through my mind of what I had just done. I had summoned a magic so strong that I almost couldn't believe it was real, and there was only one reason for it. My mind latched onto the answer before darkness took me.

Kip.

Roane dragged me up off the ground, grasping my shoulders, forcing me to look at him. Behind him, I could see Harley and Kip, and my mind relaxed. Knowing she had gotten through the fray with the pigs filled me with relief and let my muscles relax at least a small amount.

"I don't know what you did," Roane said to me when I sat back down on the altar, his eyes wide as he shook his head, "but you killed everything but us for a good mile around. It also managed to put you in a daze for the last hour. You weren't asleep, but you haven't acknowledged any of us. You had me worried."

"You know it will take more than a War Pig to stop me." My forced laugh fell flat.

"I don't have any experience with one exploding quite like that."

"What's the aftermath?"

"I haven't gone far to explore because I didn't want to leave you or the women alone, but we are safe here, for now at least. I've found some edible plants. Here." He held out a handful of leaves and small vegetables that resembled bell peppers. "Eat these."

I nodded and locked eyes with Kip. There was a strange emotion behind those eyes. She'd heard what I'd said to the Pig, and wanted to know what the hell it meant. I turned away and the moment passed. There was too much hinging on what was happening between us, more than she even knew, and I couldn't face it now. I lay back on the altar, tasting the bitter vegetables, determined that one day I would drag her into my room in my castle and show her exactly what I'd meant. She would have to know soon. But not now.

9

*K*ip "May I suggest you invest in a large map of this place and put little red pins in all the places seething with icky monsters like that one?" I said as we put the swamp behind us.

Everyone was soaking wet and smelled of War Pig and dank, the horses were dripping, their heads sagging, and Stryder was looking less than regal with his hair plastered to his neck and his wings trailing bits of swamp scum as we went. I had officially had my fill of this particular adventure.

"There are no maps," Stryder replied.

"Of course there aren't. Because why would there be? We're in the land of the fairies – Fae, sorry, Fae – why would we possibly need something as mundane as a helpful piece of paper to let us know where the hell we are?"

"You learn as you go. The Land of Sidhe is to each person what they've seen and experienced of it. A map is only a concept. It doesn't mean anything and it controls you, tells you what to think or experience. When you trust yourself and move on your own, it becomes a part of you and you don't need anything else telling you where to go."

I blinked at him a few times, swung my eyes over to Harley, and then looked back at Stryder.

"Well, when you put it like *that*."

I had to keep going. There really wasn't any choice. Mac's death couldn't be in vain and after the horror I'd witnessed with the Bogles, I knew there would be many more brutal deaths if this war didn't come to an end. I'd made my commitment to the cause and to Stryder. Not knowing where in the living hell I was, how to get back to the portal, or how to use it if I ever did find it, just compounded the situation. I was in this for the long haul.

My wave of forced optimism was rewarded by us coming over a rocky hill and looking down over a lush, green valley below. If we were back in my own realm, I'd expect to hear birds chirping and possibly squirrels getting into races with each other as they bounded from tree to tree. Possibly Snow White singing blissfully somewhere in the distance and thinking a nice, juicy apple sounded lovely. Instead, it was quiet.

We'd climbed back up onto the horses and Stryder guided us slowly down the side of the hill toward the green leaves. I wriggled closer to him. There were still some doubts in my mind about whether or not trusting him was really in my best interest. But I was in a position of having to choose between relying on him and having to face this twisted fairy tale on my own. I might not be ready to totally trust Stryder again, but it was an easy decision. The Grimm Brothers didn't have shit on this place.

"I'm probably not going to like the answer you give me no matter what it is, but I'm going to ask anyway," I said when we made it past the tree line and it was still eerily quiet around us. "Should I be worried that I'm not hearing or seeing anybody around here?"

Stryder shook his head.

"No. The inhabitants of the Woodland Realm are shy. They rarely come out to engage with travelers. Even if you encounter them, they're usually uninterested in interacting. It's just their way. Don't let it offend you."

"Why would it offend me?" I asked.

"You seemed very concerned about it," Stryder said.

"I was *concerned* because I thought this might be a War Pig situation and we were about to be retaliated against for every bacon cheeseburger that has ever been eaten, not because they didn't rush out to welcome us."

If I didn't know Stryder any better, I would have thought he chuckled.

We continued on for another hour and then Stryder pulled Thunder to a stop.

"We'll rest here for a while," he said.

"Stryder, the horses are exhausted. The women are exhausted. We should go ahead and make camp for the night. We'll get a good night's sleep and then be ready to go again first thing in the morning," Roane said.

I could feel Stryder tense in front of me. He didn't like having any of us, including Roane, trying to change his vision for the journey. Unfortunately for him, his vision for the journey didn't take into account two human women who already felt like we had been run into the ground. We weren't going to make it much longer. Finally, Stryder nodded.

"Fine," he said. "But if we're going to stop for more than a short break, we need to continue on through the next glade. The forest is thicker on the other side and will provide better cover during the night."

I didn't know how far that was, exactly, but at least having a plan for when we'd stop was the boost I needed to keep me from sliding off the side of the horse and making my own camp wherever I landed. The trip through the next glade didn't take as long as I feared and soon we'd stopped. The grateful horses stretched and shook their heads when Stryder and Roane removed their loads, then wandered into the distance to eat and rest.

Roane and Stryder built up a fire and spread out the very slim food resources that had survived the trip through the swamp. They added some of the plants we'd gathered and we sat to eat. We'd gotten through much of it when I noticed Stryder pick up a piece of vine that caught my attention. I remembered it from one of the books Mac read and reached out to stop him.

"Don't eat that," I said.

"I'm still hungry," Stryder said. "The Woodlands have edible plants. We'll collect more food tomorrow."

"The Woodlands might have plenty of edible plants, like I'm sure lots of places in the Land of Sidhe do, but that isn't one of them. It's poisonous."

He looked incredulously at the plant.

"It's a climber vine," he said. "Everyone who travels through these realms eats it."

I shook my head.

"No. That's not a climber vine. It's a moonstalk. It looks very similar, but that plant is extremely toxic. One bite is enough to incapacitate a man. More than that and it can kill you," I told him.

"You've never even been here. I've traveled through these realms extensively. I think I know more about the plants than you do."

"You think you know more about everything than everybody," Harley said.

I pointed at her. "That. Usually it's just infuriating. This could be dangerous. I read about plants in one of the books Mac loved. I didn't realize at the time they were real, but I got pretty familiar with what was in them. And that"—I turned to point my finger at the green shoot still clutched in his hand—"is a moonstalk."

Stryder pulled the vine back and looked at it. Finally, he tossed it to the side.

"Fine," he said. "I won't eat it."

My chest swelled and I beamed with accomplishment at actually being able to help him. After all the times he had saved my skin, it seemed like time I was able to reciprocate a little. We finished eating and Harley stood.

"Is there a creek or anything around here?" she asked. "I'd really like to rinse off a bit."

"There's a pond," Roane told her. "I can take you."

They looked at each other and the offer to go along with her disappeared from my mouth. I wasn't about to interfere with what was building between them. Roane and Harley disappeared into the forest and I helped Stryder build camp for the night. We crafted two shelters out of the bending branches of clusters of trees and blankets, and put everything that had been strapped to the horses inside. When we were finished, I sat down beside the fire with him again.

His wing flickered beside me, like a tired muscle that spasms to try to release the built-up energy. I felt the urge to touch it. Out of the corner of his eye Stryder noticed me looking and stretched the wing toward me. I gasped, an unexpected thrill rushing through me at the sight of the powerful expansion of himself. When they were bound up, I hadn't put a tremendous amount of thought into his wings. In the back of my mind, I knew they were there, but they weren't something that went through my thoughts often. Now that I saw them, there was no doubt they would never be far from my mind. They were undoubtedly the sexiest thing I'd ever seen.

My hand lifted almost involuntarily and I ran my fingertips along the edge. It felt muscular and leathery, but warm and alive. It twitched slightly beneath my touch and Stryder's eyes met mine. The moment was intense, the shedding of the last of the barrier between the human world and this one feeling intimate. I moved closer to him and brushed my palm along the flat part of his wing. The sensation became too much and I let my hand drop, falling silent for several seconds before I spoke.

"Can I ask you something?" I asked.

"If I said no, would that erase the question you just asked?"

"You've had a long day, so I'm going to let your sass go this time. I want to know about what you said in the swamp."

"What did I say in the swamp?" he asked.

"You said I was yours."

The words were harder to get out of my throat than I'd have liked them to be, and the gruff sound he made in his didn't make me feel better.

"You are my responsibility," he said.

"That's not what you meant."

"Of course it is."

"You said they couldn't take what was made for you," I said.

These words were even harder to say. They came out sounding powdery and uncertain. I couldn't have heard him wrong, but there was too much meaning behind that comment for me to understand. Stryder looked into my eyes and my heart started beating faster. My breath came in little gasps, but I struggled to keep it steady, to stop him from knowing how he affected me.

"I was talking about my court," Stryder said. "The Blood Court was made into what it is by my parents and passed to me. The Summer Queen is trying to take it from me like she's trying to take power of the other courts."

I shook my head. "You weren't talking to the queen or even to any of her soldiers. You were talking about me, Stryder. What did you mean?"

"I'm not going to talk about this right now, Kip."

"Why not?"

"I thought you were tired. You should change and get some sleep."

"I want to know what you were talking about," I insisted.

"It doesn't matter," Stryder responded, trying to brush me off.

"Whether something matters to me or not is really not up to you. I agreed to come here with you, to help *you*, and you won't even be honest with me."

"Don't you think there's already enough to be thinking about? Why add something else right now?"

Frustration replaced all the warm feelings I'd been having toward him and my eyes narrowed into a piercing glare.

"You know, you're right. I am *really* tired."

Storming away into the shelter would have been a lot more meaningful if it had led to me actually falling asleep. It definitely didn't. Instead, I spent the next few hours flopping around trying to get my brain to quiet down enough to rest. Harley tried valiantly to stay awake with me, but it wasn't long before she drifted to sleep. Overheated and still struggling with my tangled thoughts, I decided to step out of the shelter for some fresh air. Tossing my nightgown aside, I tugged on clothes and shoes to prepare for the potential of encountering one of the creatures of the Woodland Realm. They might not be eager to interact, but that didn't mean they needed to see me wandering around in my pajamas.

THE AIR FELT cool and damp with dew when I stepped out and filled my lungs with it. It was enough to settle some of my nerves, but only seconds later a sound caught my attention and jolted me right back to my fear. The muffled shouting and sound of grappling came from only a few yards away. I took a step toward it and my eyes finally adjusted enough to notice movement. It was Stryder. Two men held him on either side and a strap of leather gagged him as they dragged him away.

"Stryder!" I screamed out before thinking.

The men didn't pause and soon disappeared into the darkness of the trees beyond. I remembered what he had said about being alone, but it didn't matter. There was no time to get Roane. He needed help. Without another thought, I took off after them.

10

Stryder

After my tense conversation with Kip, it was hard to fall asleep. When I finally did, it felt like I'd only been resting for a few minutes when someone shaking me brought me back awake. This wasn't a gentle shaking, a careful gesture meant to wake me up carefully. This was rough, almost violent shaking demanding my immediate attention. At first it seemed like a nightmare, then an attack. It wasn't until I heard Harley's voice that I realized something was wrong.

"Stryder! Stryder, wake up."

Her eyes were wild when I looked up at her. She immediately grabbed me by the wrist and yanked me up into a sitting position.

"Harley? What are you doing?"

"Wake up. Kip is gone."

That was all I needed to hear. I was immediately wide awake, fear coursing through my body.

"What do you mean Kip is gone?" I asked.

"I'd say it's a fairly self-explanatory statement. She's gone. She's not here. We need to find her."

"Where did she go? How long has she been gone?"

"If I knew where she went, I'd be going after her. As much as it offends you and your masculinity, I am not one of the people in your life who need you. We're wasting time," she growled.

"Harley," Roane said from the other side of the shelter. "What's going on?"

Her face softened in a way I knew she wouldn't want anyone to notice. She stepped over me to get to him.

"I thought I heard Kip shouting for Stryder a little while ago. But it was coming from outside and I had been really deeply asleep, so I figured it was a dream. I just woke up and she's not in the shelter. She's nowhere around."

I got up and dressed.

"You heard her calling for me?" I asked. "Outside the shelter?"

She looked over her shoulder and nodded. I met eyes with Roane. There was no question about what happened and that meant we were rapidly losing time.

"Pack everything," I said. "I'll get the horses."

Harley followed me as I ducked out of the shelter.

"What's going on?" she asked. "What do you know?"

"You said you heard her calling for me from outside, but now she's gone. I talked to her about it not being safe for her to be alone at any time. As stubborn as she might be, she understood. She wouldn't just wander away."

Harley scoffed, but I ignored her and started breaking down the outside of the camp.

"Because you told her not to?" she asked. "You really think you have power over everybody, don't you?"

"Not because I told her not to. Because while she might be difficult and want to do things I ask her not to just to piss me off, she isn't stupid. You heard her. She wasn't comfortable with not knowing where we were and not having a map to follow.

Do you think that translates into her walking out of her shelter and roaming out into the darkness just for fun?"

"I would really prefer you to not past-tense her," Harley said, her voice starting to tremble.

I drew in a breath. "She wouldn't just walk away," I emphasize. "It's not in her character."

"Don't pretend to know her," Harley said through gritted teeth.

I whip around to face her, gripping the tools in my hand so tight they cut into my palm. "Don't pretend to be the only one who does."

Roane came out of the shelter with the bags and dipped into the other to gather the women's belongings. I called out to the horses and within a few moments heard them running toward me. The sound of Thunder's hooves against the ground reminded me of Kip's promise to tease me for his name. I felt my heart squeeze and hoped I'd have the opportunity to listen to the taunts.

"Can you make him tell me what happened to Kip?" Harley asked when Roane carried the rest of the bags out to us and started breaking down the shelter.

"The Summer Fae," I said. "They came for her. There's no way she would leave alone, which means something lured her away. Something was pressing enough to get her to leave without waking anybody up. Harley said she heard her calling for me. Summer Fae used their glamour to look like me so she would follow. I don't know what they did, but they got her away from here and now they have their hands on her. Which means she is in serious danger."

"How serious?" Harley asked.

"The Summer Fae have Kip under their control," Roane told her. "They have taken her so they can bring her to their queen to be used in the war."

"Then we go to her. We go to the Summer Court and confront this bitch."

I shook my head as I tied the bags onto Thunder.

"No. They wouldn't bring her directly to the Summer Court. That's what we'd be expecting them to do. They wouldn't want to be so obvious. They're holding her somewhere. They're going to want to lay low and stay out of detection for a while until they think we're not on their trail, and then go for the court. They took her somewhere they can keep her hidden and secure."

"Where?"

"I don't know, but we have to find her as soon as we can."

"It hasn't been too long," Harley said. "They couldn't have gotten very far. Unless they flew. I don't know how fast you people can use those wings of yours."

"They wouldn't fly," Roane reassured her. "It would be difficult to conceal Kip dangling under them as they headed across the land."

"We just have to search," I said. "And hope we figure it out."

11

Kip The overwhelming darkness didn't change much when my eyes fluttered open and didn't magically go away when they began to adjust and focus either. I tried to move my arm, but the soreness and sharp pain in my chest stopped me from doing much more than wiggling my back against the wall. At least that gave me some perspective.

The room I was in was small, cramped and almost empty. In one corner was a makeshift commode, and across from that was what looked like iron bars. Outside the bars I could see flickering light, like an open flame. The floor was cobblestone, nicked and rounded by the years, and covered in dirt and grime. I lay on what felt like a wooden board on the floor, a roach passing just inches from my face. I pushed my arms against the ground again, forcing myself up to my knees as the pain seared through the back of my arm. It was bruised badly and dried blood stained my shirt and crusted under my nose, telling me that at some point I had been hit.

I listened for the sound of Stryder or Harley or Roane. I

knew I was alone, but I wanted to hold out hope. Maybe one of them was in a cell near me and we could figure out what to do next together. Even as I tried to convince myself of that, I knew it wasn't true. The Summer Fae who had lured me away from the camp revealed themselves as soon as I was in their grip. None of the others were with me and I didn't know how long I'd been gone. They might not have even realized I was gone.

I inched closer to the bars and tried to peer through them. There were only three cells, one across from me and one to the side. Both were empty sans the skeleton of some unfortunate soul in one. The walls curved sharply in another direction and the flame came from just behind it.

From far away, I heard voices murmuring. Two deep growling voices spoke in low tones, and I could just make out a phrase.

"...if not, we get rid of her."

"We can't do that. Ajeka would have our heads."

"She'd never know we found her. I'm not putting my skin on the line for some human woman. If she's too much trouble, she'll just disappear."

The words sent a shiver down my spine, and I recoiled to the board when I saw shadows moving toward me. Two Fae men stood at the bars of my cell and peered in at me and through my mostly closed eyes, I could see the taller one snicker and turn to the other.

"Six hours, and then I'll be down to relieve you. She might be out the entire time. Gartha hit her pretty hard in the back of the head."

"Are you sure she's still alive?"

"She is. For now. I can see her breathing. We have to keep her alive until she has fulfilled her purpose."

They laughed. They laughed at the idea that my life was so easily snuffed out if I wasn't what they wanted. I had never had more reason to be scared in my entire life, but instead, I felt rage. An anger that filled up inside me so far that I felt like I might burst. It took everything I had to not move, not to make a sound.

The tall one walked away and the shorter turned his back to me, moving to the wall and pulling up a chair. He sat down heavily and yawned.

I had to get out of there.

The one pressing issue standing in my way was that I had absolutely no idea how to do it. Being held captive in something somewhere between a cage and a cell—possibly underground, possibly not—wasn't something I'd picked up along the way in my life. Maybe it was a later module in the first aid course I'd abandoned. Possibly part of emergency preparedness.

The man I assumed was supposed to be guarding me didn't seem to be paying a tremendous amount of attention. This gave me more confidence. It would be far more difficult to attempt a daring escape from somewhere if every move was being closely monitored. Looking around the room to gain my bearings, I tried to decide what to do first. There weren't many options. I went to the window and tried to squeeze through the bars. My face squished through, but that was about it. They apparently had an exceptionally small amount of trust in this...prison? Is that where I was?

If so, maybe they had exactly right amount of trust in the type of people who would usually end up in here. Only, it shouldn't be me.

It was utterly futile, but I turned to the other side and tried to go through the bars again. My time in the land hadn't taught me much so far, but one thing I had picked up was not to automatically believe everything was as it seemed. It was entirely possible there was a trick to getting out of the cell and I just needed to try everything that came to mind until I found it. One of those *trust in yourself and all you need will come to you* or *it was all inside you all along* situations.

When attempting to change my state of matter to toothpaste consistency and get out through the window didn't pan out, I went back to pacing the space. Something had to jump out at me.

Shit. No. Rephrase that. I definitely didn't want anything to jump out at me.

Something had to *occur* to me at some point. I just needed to look and think. This was just like a sparsely-decorated, fantasy-themed escape room.

It just sucked I was really bad at escape rooms. The only time I did one, I'd decided to forgo a team and the owner had to come rescue me. Not a resounding endorsement for my skills.

"I don't know if you should have brought her here."

The sound of the voices coming from outside the cell came back, making the hair stand up on the back of my neck and goosebumps break out along my arms.

"Where else would we have brought her?" another voice hissed.

"We should have brought her straight to Ajeka. This woman will be what guarantees victory for our queen. She will protect and save her. Every minute without her, Ajeka is at risk. Do you want her to be harmed and know she could have been protected if only we had brought this human woman directly to her rather than hiding her here?"

"And do you want to be the one to stand before your queen and explain to her that we had her right in the palms of our hands, but because we went directly to the Summer Court, Stryder was able to track us down? Are you going to be the one who disappoints and angers her that way? The King of Ashes will not relent. If we went straight to the Summer Court, he would find us and take this woman back. He would be the ruin of the queen and the war."

I beamed with pride, strengthened and encouraged by the

words. They really did fear Stryder. *The King of Ashes.* That had a forceful, sexy ring to it.

"Not for long. There are others waiting for him. Now that we have her in our control, there's no need to be careful. They will be eager to destroy him and Roane."

And that sent me smashing right back down to the ground. This was a roller coaster of emotions and I wanted to get the fuck off. Now King of Ashes was not sounding anywhere near as impressive. It sounded foreboding.

"I will still feel better when we are able to deliver this woman to our queen and know she will be there to perform her function. There are too many who have been waiting for her. We won't be able to hide her for long. People have had to leave the Land of the Sidhe because of her. Others have lost their lives. Some have done both."

Silence fell for a few tense seconds.

"Mac knew what he was getting himself into. He knew what she meant."

I must have gasped or made some other noise in response to what they said because one of the men silenced the other. In the quiet that followed, I could imagine them straining toward the cell, listening for more.

"Have you checked on her?" one finally asked.

I tossed myself to the floor and assumed my best unconscious look. An instant later, footsteps came to the door. Someone hovered just outside for what felt like hours. I'd turned my back to the door, which concealed my face in the darkness enough I felt confident opening my eyes a small slit. Inches in front of me was the stone wall of the cell. Channeling my inner Aladdin, I used one finger to poke one of the stones. It didn't move. Nope. That wasn't going to get me out, either.

When the footsteps finally moved away, I let out a breath I hadn't realized I was holding. Fear made my skin feel cold and brought tears to the corners of my eyes. I wished Stryder was there with me. The thought went through my mind so automatically it surprised me. I felt warmth in my chest and a calming sensation going down my back when I thought of him and realized with stunned surprise that I was truly and genuinely beginning to trust him.

12

Stryder

"Where could they have brought her?" Harley asked.

I finished tightening the last of the bags to Ominous Thunder. I'd tied them down particularly securely, not wanting any risk of them moving or loosening while we searched. We couldn't afford any distractions.

"I don't know," I told her.

"That's it?" she asked. "You just don't know?"

"Do enemy armies frequently offer carefully organized and footnoted descriptions of their plans to make sure everyone is on the same page?" I snapped. "This isn't a game, Harley."

"Are you sure? Because it sure feels a hell of a lot like we're doing some Capture the Kip shit and they are most definitely winning."

"They aren't winning," I growled at her through gritted teeth.

This woman truly drove me right to the edge. Just when I started to think I might be able to see through the harsh exterior she put up and find ways to appreciate her if not like her,

Harley managed to put on clear display exactly how exasperating she could be. And not exasperating in the way that Kip infuriated me, but still made me want more. This was just in the way that if I wasn't fully aware of the close bond she had with Kip, I'd have abandoned Harley two days ago.

"Stryder, we need to focus," Roane said. "Harley, when you heard Kip calling for Stryder, could you tell where it was coming from, other than just outside the shelter?"

Harley stared at him for a few seconds and I realized she was thinking, focusing on him to let the rest of the world disappear.

"No," she said.

It was a flatline, a disappointment after a buildup I thought might bring us somewhere.

"No? Nothing?" Roane asked.

"It was the middle of the night!" Harley exclaimed. "I was still most of the way asleep and I didn't even know if it was actually real or not, much less that it would have something to do with Kip going missing. Excuse me if I didn't hop up and do a forensic artist sketch of the area to pinpoint the exact location."

"You are lashing out at Stryder for not knowing where Kip could have gone. But you're the only one with any information about when she left. Can't you think of something?" Roane asked.

Her face darkened but a splash of color across the tops of her cheekbones was an illustration of the tension building inexplicably and unescapably between them. If anyone else had snapped at her like that, Harley might have swallowed them whole. But because it was Roane, that fury was tempered with hurt. Of course, that meant the reaction had the potential of being even more furious, so I braced myself.

"I...don't...know," she finally said. "*You* figure it out."

The slow, shaking staccato of her voice was worse than if she had started screaming. Roane stepped up closer to her.

"Close your eyes. Pretend you're in the shelter again. Where did you hear her voice? Did it seem like she was behind you or in front of you?"

She thought again. I knew my best friend was trying to carefully guide her, to bring to the surface that one small detail that could be instrumental in finding Kip. But I was losing patience. Minutes were ticking past and with every second she was gone, I knew she was in more danger. This wasn't the time to hold hands and commune with each other. We needed to be searching.

Before I had a chance to move, Harley's head suddenly snapped up. She looked to the opposite side of the area where we'd set up camp.

"Over there," she pointed. "It sounded like she was shouting from over there."

"Come on," I commanded.

I rushed in that direction and, after spending some time searching, noticed scrape marks in the soft soil, headed in one direction. They were faint, but it was enough. I ran back to Thunder and jumped onto his back. Even the pain deep in my still-recovering leg didn't register anymore. I didn't care about anything but finding Kip. Thunder seemed to sense my urgency as he burst into a run. Roane and Harley were still standing where I'd left them. I believed they would follow me, but even if they didn't, I wouldn't stop. Not until I found her and knew she was safe.

Then I'd deal with the people who took her.

The trail in the dirt faded and I pulled Thunder to a stop. A few minutes later, Roane and Harley rushed up behind me.

"What do you see?" Roane asked.

I shook my head as I jumped down and searched for the impression again.

"Nothing," I said. "That's the problem. There was a trail."

"A trail?" Harley asked.

"In the dirt. A rut, like someone being dragged. Then it just ends," I said.

"Maybe they were dragging Kip?" Roane asked.

"Then what? Why does it just end? What happened in this spot?" I asked.

I looked around at the trees, at the ground beneath my feet. I didn't say what I was looking for. Putting voice to the fear of seeing fresh blood or wayward strands of vibrant red hair would be too much. My mouth stayed quiet as my eyes scoured the area.

"There are hoofprints." Roane pointed. "Are they yours?"

"No. Thunder stopped where he is."

We looked at each other and without another word mounted our horses again. My urgency made me want to race through the trees, but I forced myself to lead Thunder slowly so we wouldn't miss anything that might guide us. We followed the hoofprints until they turned from a consistent, easy to follow trail into a tangle of prints, some deeper, some smeared until they blended with others. It looked like the horse that had come this way had gotten spooked. Or that several had met in this spot and gone in different directions.

My head was spinning. Behind me, Harley and Roane were back to their discussion. It vacillated between bickering at each other and something more familiar and comfortable, something close enough to flirting it made me uncomfortable. I blocked it out. Closing my focus in, I let myself think only of my surroundings and anything that might tell me what happened to Kip after the Summer Fae got her away from the shelter.

My stomach flipped and my heart squeezed painfully in my chest when I thought of them manipulating her that way. Guilt made bile rise up in my throat. She left because she thought she was following me. They chose exactly what they knew would bring her away from the safety of the rest of the group without going for help. If she thought either of the others were in danger, she would have immediately come to me. She never would have tried to follow them alone. But because it was me, she was willing to go. I was her source of security and it had been used against her.

Suddenly a sense of peace settled over me. It was an odd sensation, almost palpable in how it affected my body. My heart slowed and the fear tingling on my skin settled. It felt like I was close to Kip, like I could reach out and touch her somewhere around me. The warmth she generated spread through my belly and up through my chest, seeming to tug me as it guided me in another direction.

I couldn't explain it, but the feeling was irresistible. The intensity of the draw made it so I couldn't deny it. Grasping Thunder's harness, I let the feeling pull me along, hoping in the end this wasn't another manipulation. I hoped it was my Fated Mate calling out to me.

13

*K*ip The man was still sitting in the chair near the door to my cell. I had poked a few more of the stones throughout the room for good measure and tested along the bottom of the walls to make sure whoever had been in here before me hadn't started a tunnel I could continue working on. Every time I glanced over at the door, I could see the man's legs sticking out from the chair and knew my options were slim.

I couldn't stop thinking about what they'd said about Mac. It didn't make any sense, but it made my stomach twist and bubble in that way that told me something wasn't right. A few others had come by to chat with my guard and the snippets of conversations I caught only confirmed my personal safety was getting thinner and thinner by the minute. While the resounding opinion of most of the men swarming around whatever this place was meant keeping me alive until they could deliver me like a hand-picked cherry to the queen, it wasn't unanimous. Some felt the job had been botched from the beginning and they should just cut their losses. Others felt like it was too much trouble pitting themselves against Stryder in such a personal way.

My guard was playing devil's advocate, interchangeably arguing for both sides, and that only made him more ominous.

Maybe he would sleep soon. If he finally gave in to the deep, rumbling yawns he kept letting out, I might be able to fish the key to the cell out of his pocket and free myself. Except, he sat too far away for me to reach a key so that was out. It occurred to me I wasn't going to be able to get out of the cell by myself. He was going to have to do it for me, which meant I had to get him to come into the cell with me. It was my only chance of escape.

Time passed. How much, I didn't know, but it felt like an eternity. I drifted in and out of a dreamless sleep because there was nothing else to do. My body ached with exhaustion, and when I awoke again, the guard was snoring loudly. I had to act now, so that he would be disoriented waking up so suddenly. A hasty plan formed in my mind and I steeled myself for what I had to do.

I began to cough, then gag loudly. I shook my legs violently and made gurgling sounds like I was choking to death. The guard snapped awake and I briefly saw panic cross his face as he began to fumble with the keys to the cell. A moment later the door was open and he was heading toward me. He leaned down, bent at the waist and I could smell his unwashed body odor and a faint, sharp, whiskey-like smell. He opened a mouth filled with rotten teeth and began to speak when I shoved my foot directly into his groin and grabbed the lapels of his jacket, yanking him forward.

His balance temporarily lost due to the ball-crunching heel kick, I was able to use his momentum to smash his head into the wall behind me, rolling out of the way when he fell. Snatching the keyring from his waistband, I ran for the door, but just as I crossed the threshold, a hand gripped my ankle. I tried to shake it away to no avail and he pulled himself toward me. I grabbed the door of the cell and swung hard, smashing his face and arm and sending a stream of blood pouring from his nose. I slammed it again and again, until his body stopped moving and I was positive he was either unconscious or dead. He was still breathing, but I wouldn't feel particularly bad if he suddenly stopped. Instead, I shoved his head and arm back in the cell and shut it tightly, hearing the click of the locking mechanism.

I felt my way around the walls until I rounded the corner and could see by torchlight. It seemed like I was at the base of a winding staircase, and something pricked in the back of my mind, just out of reach. Something familiar. Carefully I began to move forward, up the rising stairs, ready to duck back down at the sound of anyone ahead of me. But nothing came, and I walked for quite some time before a sharp stream of daylight ahead of me broke through one of the walls. I tried not to hurry to it, in case I was seen, but I could barely contain myself. The fresh air coming in from beyond that crack in the wall was rejuvenating and the light was brighter than anything I had seen in hours.

I kneeled down to get closer to it and noticed I could see out of it. The sun was on the other side of wherever I was, but it was still flooding the area with light. It must be the middle of the day now, heading toward evening. I wondered where Stryder was, and if he had any idea where I was. Looking out, I could see that I was actually several floors above ground, and across from me was a tower. The land around it was lush and surrounded by a wooded area, and the nagging feeling of something familiar pricked at me again, but this time harder. I scrambled in my mind to catch it, and all at once it hit me.

The Towers, a story Mac had told me, one I'd thought he made up or read in some old book, but was really from his home. The Towers, where two brothers, framed for the murder of their father the king, were held. The Towers, where... what was it? One of them escaped, and the other died because... because... Oh, it was right there. Right on the edge of my mind.

Suddenly, like water rushing down a pipe, sweeping everything in its way with it, the memory came back at me, and it was like I was standing in the bookstore again. Mac was there, and the story he wound was fascinating. One of the brothers, he had said, escaped. Not by climbing out the top of the tower, but by a secret door. In the bottom. In a cell.

The skeleton.

I turned on my heel and ran, cursing myself the entire time, knowing that if this wasn't right that I could be wasting the one good opportunity I had at getting to the top and maybe out a window. My feet pounded on the steps until I was suddenly back in the cell room. In my old cell, the guard was still out, blood pooling under his head. I turned my attention to the cell with the skeleton and tried to open the door.

"Dammit," I muttered under my breath as it caught, locked tight. I grabbed at the keyring, trying each one until finally one of them turned, and with a considerable amount of effort, I opened the door.

The skeleton lay against a corner of the room, almost sitting up. Like a magnet, I was drawn to him, and as I reached him, I saw one finger of his left hand was extended. I followed the pointing finger to the other side of the cell. Nothing seemed out of place at first, and then as I tried to sweep away decades of dust and grime away from the wall, I saw it. A keyhole.

I grabbed at the keyring again and began pushing each key in, but none of them seemed to fit. Just as the last key stubbornly refused to open it, I heard the sounds of the guard slowly waking up. I looked over to see him rolling around, gingerly, as he tried to figure out what the hell had happened. Panicked, I went back to the skeleton and searched it again for anything I might have missed. I tried to focus, to zone out everything else, even the now rising bellow of the guard as he started to come to and notice that his arm might be broken in several places.

As if my eyes knew where it was all along, they zeroed in on something dark and gray, barely perceptible against the bleak blackness of the cell. Deep in the corner, behind the skeletal remains, was a key, and I grabbed for it. Snatching it up and running back to the wall, I shoved it into the keyhole.

"Come on, come on, come on, come on..." I muttered under my breath as I turned it.

Something clinked in the wall. A small shift in the stones appeared, and light came through the crack. I shoved on them hard, and it creaked open, enough for me to get through. Taking the key with me, I slammed it shut, hopefully ensuring that no one could follow me.

I was in a long hallway, and torches, unlit, lined the walls. I felt my way down until I felt the walls stop and a new hallway crossed the one I was on. I had to make a choice about which direction to go, and had just steeled myself to move when an arm wrapped around me and pulled me backward, off my feet and against a wall, while blinding light suddenly filled my eyes.

14

Stryder

"Kip, Kip, it's me," I shouted as she struggled in my grasp. Her eyes were wild and searching, but eventually they met mine and she stopped, relief flooded her face and she embraced me, nearly singeing her arm as she threw it around my neck. She squeezed me tightly and I could tell she was very faintly crying into my shoulder.

"Hey, hey, it's okay. It's okay. I've got you," I said. She peeled herself away from me and looked around the maze-like crossway. I had no idea where she had come from. I'd thought at first she was another enemy to eliminate on my search for her. "Where did you come from?" I asked.

"There was a cell. Oh, God, Mac, Mac knew it. He told me a story about two brothers, and two towers, and one escaped, and it was real. It was real, Stryder. And I found the key and I got out and all of a sudden you were here."

She was babbling but I thought I understood her. I knew that story too, from years before as a child. I had fallen asleep to it many times as a child. She was still half-talking, half-gesturing the story when I decided I had to interrupt her.

"Look, there will be plenty of time to tell me what happened later. For right now, we have to go," I said.

"Harley!"

From behind me, Roane and Harley arrived and Kip threw her arms around her. They embraced for a moment as Roane came close to me, holding his torch out toward one of the darkened hallways.

"We have to move, Stryder. I am glad you found her, but we have to get out of here while we can. I remember how we got in if you will follow me," he told me in a muted whisper.

I nodded. Roane had always had an excellent sense of direction, and his ability in mazes was legendary from his childhood. It was one of the reasons he made such a great second for me. I knew as long as Roane was around I was never truly lost. Roane stepped past the women and they broke their embrace. Kip fell back toward me as Harley stepped closer to Roane, their natural chemistry becoming more apparent as we paired off.

Kip hugged close to me as we wound our way through the narrow tunnels, and after a few moments, I felt the fear beginning to return to her. Our connection was so close I could feel it raising the hair on my own arms, and I looked over to her, catching her eyes and smiling, trying to ease her fear. A mild smile crossed her lips, one cautioned with the experience she had just had.

"So, how did you find me?" she asked, breaking the silence.

I debated how to respond to her, whether now was the time to tell her the full truth. Should I temper it with a half truth? Before I could really think about it, the words came flowing out of my mouth.

"I could sense you. Our... connection. It's extremely strong, and I could start to home in on your location."

"Like a game of hot and cold?" she asked, nudging me with her hip.

"Yeah, something like that," I met her eyes again. "I followed the feeling until it lead me to this part of the realm. I have never been here before, but it seemed familiar for some reason. We skirted around until we saw an entrance to this bunker area and I could feel you down there. So we went. I just happened to be a few feet ahead of Roane and Harley when you just showed up in front of me."

She nodded but kept silent. We walked along for a little while longer before Roane stopped cold. He turned back to look at me and pushed his torch into the wall, killing the flame.

"Someone is in the tunnels," he said, "ahead of us. They must know she is missing and that she is down here."

I killed my flame as well and we all backed against the wall. In the distance, we heard the sounds of men shouting and running. The one or two of them that we had encountered on our way down into the maze had been no problem, but this sounded like many more. I sidled closer to Roane so we were in whispering distance. He had his eyes closed and his lips were moving silently.

"How many?" I asked.

"Sounds like eight. Possibly nine. No less than six. They are splitting off to look for her. If we go quickly on my cue, we might make it out behind them."

He looked to me for approval. Roane was a hardened and talented warrior, but he still respected the hierarchy. It was my decision to make, and I nodded. I trusted Roane and his instincts. Without another word, he grabbed Harley's arm and bolted around a corner. I did the same with Kip and we ran as softly as possible, following Roane. Suddenly, he stopped in his tracks and looked back to me.

There was a silent conversation between us, the kind two people who know each other well and trust each other implicitly can have. Behind his eyes I could read the strategy, and I knew it was right. Kip wouldn't like it, especially after being away from everyone for so long, but it was the best way to survive.

"We have to split up. They are all around us and if we separate, we can meet back up outside," I said to Kip and Harley.

"What?" Harley said incredulously.

I got the impression that had the suggestion come from Roane the edge in her voice would be a lot less sharp.

"If we split up, we can move faster," Roane said. "You come with me, and Kip and Stryder will go the other way. If we get out before you, we will wait in the tree line. If you get there first..."

"Kip, let's go," I said, not waiting to hear the rest of it.

I knew what he was going to say and I hated it, but he was right.

Roane was already inching his head around one corner and looked back again. I grabbed Kip by the arm and we took off in the other direction, rounding a corner just as the shouts of Fae guards entered the hall we had previously been in. I could sense the exit ahead of us, the fresh air beckoning us from the near distance.

15

Kip The heat of torches was filling the tunnels with thick air that made it harder to breathe. Smoke wafted into hallways and around corners from the men's torches, and Stryder kept pushing us ahead and then stopping, using his arm to hold me back and force me against a wall. The voices seemed like they were everywhere and I couldn't help but worry about Harley. I knew she was as safe as she could be with Roane, not to mention how tough she was on her own, but that still didn't quell how much I didn't like splitting up.

A passageway ahead of us suddenly burst into light, and Stryder pulled us back into the shadows. I held my breath as the heavy footsteps of two Fae guards thundered past only feet away. There was shouting coming from deep in the catacombs and my fear of Harley being caught drew a lump in my throat. Stryder reached into his belt and pulled out a long knife, and I abandoned all hope that we would get out easily. There was going to be a fight at some point, it was just a matter of when.

Slowly the sound started to fade and there was an eerie silence around us. Stryder turned to look at me and put one finger over his mouth. He stepped from the safety of our shadowed corner and we began to make our way through the dark hallways. Suddenly I could smell the fresh air again, roses and lilacs and the sharp, soothing scent of pine that always made me think of Christmas. The woods must not have been far from where the entrance was, and we were inching closer to it.

We rounded a corner and I could see light, the low, lazy sunlight of early evening, coming in from a high window and farther down from a much larger opening. It must have been the door. Stryder's pace quickened and we made up the space in mere seconds. Skidding to a stop, we nearly fell over one another as we stumbled upon the door. Two guards, silent and stoic, but both facing the other direction, were standing outside it. Stryder ushered us back behind the curve of the last wall and I breathed a long slow exhale that wanted desperately to be a scream of shock.

Stryder pushed me back against the wall and looked me deep in the eyes, calming me without words, before turning and kneeling low. He picked up a stone and threw it, sending it careening off the wall and out toward the guards. The sound of heavy footsteps following the sound reverberated off the walls. Stryder leaned back into the shadows, his knife at the ready, and when the first Fae guard came around the corner, he leapt into him, covering his mouth with the inside of one arm, and slicing through his throat with the knife.

There was very little sound, but what sound there was must have alerted the other guard that something wasn't right. His footsteps began to head toward us, and Stryder pulled the sword from the dead guard's sheath. As the second guard came around the corner, Stryder met him head on, stabbing him in the stomach with the sword and running him into the wall. The guard made a surprised yell, and Stryder buried the knife into his jaw from underneath, silencing him. Pulling the knife from the now dying guard, Stryder turned to me, grasping at my hand with his bloody fingers.

"Come on, we have to go now."

My feet responded before my coherent thoughts could. We pounded around the corner, hearing the shouts of guards from deep within the maze of hallways, now having discovered Stryder's attack. Our feet slapped hard on the ground, no longer looking for soft purchase and stealth, but slamming like madness into the cobblestones, needing only speed. I could feel the cool breeze on my slick skin as we neared it, and Stryder sheathed his knife and pulled out his sword. Whatever lay beyond that door, he wanted to be ready.

We emerged from the darkness and the heat of the bunker to the cool of the early evening with a rush of adrenaline and terror. The sounds behind us of Fae guards chasing through the catacombs to us was loud, even outside, and Stryder didn't slow his pace now that he was running through grass. I kept my own pace behind him, my head still ringing and the fresh air reminding me of wounds from hours before.

Luck had prevailed and there were no guards out here that we could see. Stryder and I made it to the tree line quickly. Just a small way into the woods, I could see the horses, and Stryder made a break for them. I started looking around wildly, hoping against hope that Roane and Harley were close by, but they were nowhere to be found. We made it to the horses and Stryder reached for me to help me get onto Thunder with him.

"Shouldn't we wait?" I asked, hesitating to grab his hand for the moment.

"No, they will catch up. I trust Roane. We have to get you out of here right now, as fast as we can."

"But how will they know where to find us? Aren't we just leaving them to fight off everyone and running away?"

"Roane can handle himself," Stryder said, "and it's not abandoning him. I am leaving his horse, he knows we need to go, and he knows where I would go from here. We have fought side by side for a long time. He will find us. But right now, you need to get on this horse so I can bring you to safety before it's too late."

I didn't like it at all, but in that moment, I made a choice to trust that Roane could protect my friend. I reached up and took Stryder's hand, barely stepping up to my toes as he lifted me easily onto the seat in front of him. Straddling the great horse, I wiggled down so that I was tucked down into Stryder's body, and despite all reason, for once I felt safe. Stryder spurred the horse into movement and after a few steps, into a great gallop.

Ducking through low branches and winding our way around or over trees, we made it a short distance before Stryder suddenly pulled on the reins and Thunder came to a stop. I opened my mouth to say something when I heard the crack of a twig in the distance. Snapping my head in that direction, I saw the movement of a large white horse.

Like a sea cresting the beach at high tide, an army of Fae men came through the woods and into the small clearing we now found ourselves in. All but one were on foot, and they all carried swords. There must have been twenty of them and I got the impression more were on their way. A smirk crossed the lips of the man on horseback and he drew his sword, laying it across his lap.

"Stryder, how unsurprised I am to see you here."

"Before you even get started," Stryder interrupted, "I have zero interest in wasting time here so you can get reinforcements ready. Either you can fight here and die, or you can let us through and pretend that you just missed us. Your choice."

The horseman laughed and gripped his sword tightly.

"I don't need reinforcements for you, Stryder. I don't even need these men here. Just me."

"Then tell them to leave."

"I would rather they watch," he said, sliding off his horse.

With a smack, his horse moved deep into the woods. Stryder slid off Thunder and pulled him behind, looking back up to me.

"If I say go, you go. Thunder will get you somewhere safe. Understand?" he asked intensely. I nodded, but he must have noticed the fear in my eyes. "It's going to be okay. Just in case."

My foot moved into the saddle, preparing to brace for the speed and intensity that I knew this horse could produce, when I noticed a sheath behind it. Sticking out of the top of the sheath was the handle of a sword, and I looked down at it. It was gold with rubies encased in the hilt. It was shorter than the sword Stryder now bore, but it felt thick and powerful as I tried to lift it with my heel. I knew that if something happened, I might need to use it and my hand closed around it in preparation. Whatever was going to come next, I needed to be ready.

16

Stryder

I took a step forward, half expecting them all to charge at once. When they didn't, I locked eyes with Elgin, their cruel leader, and he grinned. He had a plan, he always had a plan, and I just had to find a way out of it. Elgin rarely engaged in a fair battle. Right now, he had a small battalion and I had me, and a young woman who I was pretty sure had never held a weapon.

There were roughly fifteen to twenty of his men, all with swords, all young and hungry-looking. It was true that Elgin was known for being devious and cocky, but he had reason to be. Immensely talented with the sword, Elgin was the leader of a cavalry unit that had brought our own army many troubles. I had to be careful with him, and at my best, or else Kip was going to have to go it alone. I surveyed the standing army with him as they began to sheath their swords. I didn't expect them to stay that way, but at least I would get a chance for a somewhat fair fight.

Elgin stepped forward, twirling his sword in an elaborate

and unnecessary way. He did it to infuriate me and throw me off my game. Showing off like that isn't to make you look good, it's to make your opponent want to stop you. I wasn't going to bite, and instead flourished mine with a bit of drama too. The smirk on Elgin's face dropped a little, letting me know that I had gotten to him.

We circled each other for a moment, but his eyes darting toward Kip caused me to stop and circle back the other direction. He followed suit and I exhaled deeply. He was going to make the first move; people like him always did. I just had to wait and judge it.

Suddenly, he thrust, harder than I expected, and I just barely knocked it out of the way. Swinging it back around, he came at me again and I rolled to the side, swiping at his legs and meeting his sword on a downward arc. I thrust toward his stomach and Elgin sidestepped it, raising his sword up to push mine away. I spun with another swing and was met by a shoulder in my ribs. I stumbled back and tried to regain my footing as he swung at me from alternating directions, missing me by inches each time. I found my footing and jumped forward, this time taking him aback and forcing him into the defensive.

Our battle was a seesaw of classic technique, and it dawned on me that he had no intention of defeating me one on one. He was waiting, hoping to tire me out while reinforcements arrived. He was playing to my ego and my desire to personally avenge deaths I knew he had caused to my men. I had to change plans, and fast.

Elgin parried somewhat softly, a sign that he was falling into the rhythm of a sword fight and not actually paying attention as if it were life and death. This was his one weakness, and I aimed to exploit it. He would get cocky, and stop forcing forward, relying more on wearing an opponent down than risk charging and losing. I took the opportunity and slashed at his hand in a circular motion, a trick I learned long ago. The laceration was a surprise to him and he nearly dropped his sword. Anger filled his eyes and he swung at me in a complicated motion that would have deceived a lesser-trained warrior into thinking it was coming from another direction. I was able to avoid the slash and allowed his momentum to carry him too far forward. With just a small thrust, I felt the tip of my sword pierce his side, where the chainmail and armor failed to protect.

Elgin stumbled to the ground and when he found himself on his behind, looking up at me as I began to charge, his voice filled the forest.

"Charge!" he shouted, and twenty swords were suddenly unsheathed around me.

I stopped in my tracks as Elgin shuffled and rolled away from me, a Fae cavalry member taking his place. I avoided his inexpert swing and ran him through in one singular motion. The next was already on me and I knocked away his sword, elbowing him in the jaw to create some distance. I was not going to be able to win this fight without magic, but I knew I had to reserve as much energy as possible to escape.

Feeling a warm burn slowly fill my arm, I swept it out over a huddled mass of men who were making their way toward me. Pure energy, electric blue and crackling with the sound of air bubbles bursting violently all around it, shot from my hand in an arc, blowing the men backward, unconscious. The elbowed guard was regaining his footing, and I swept my sword behind his knee, cutting his leg off at the joint, and he fell backward. Sweeping the sword around, I brought it down on his neck, removing his head and spinning into another thrust to the stomach of a fellow charging Fae.

"Behind you," Kip shouted from atop the horse, and I turned to see an all-too-close blade in my vision.

I ducked instinctively and could feel the blade part my hair. I barreled into him, tackling him to the ground, building up a charge in my hand. I placed it on his chest and simultaneously blasted him with a burst of magic while using him to propel myself back into a standing position. His body went limp, and I swung the sword to catch an arm on the backswing, cutting deep into the bone and sending the Fae screaming and falling away.

I could hear crashing in the woods behind the men that were left and knew my time had run out. The reinforcements had arrived and were now creating a half circle around the battlefield. Only a few members of the original group remained now, and Elgin had gone missing, so I took the moment to breathe deeply and focus. I had a finite amount of magical energy left and no way to replenish it without rest. It wasn't enough to take out all of them, but perhaps I could use everything I had to kill or incapacitate most of them and Kip could escape. I was preparing to summon all of my power when a sound behind me forced me to turn.

Roane, Harley, and a small battalion of my own men, some of my trusted insiders, had arrived. Harley sat atop Roane's horse, but he was on foot, along with my men. The battlefield came to a standstill as our forces lined up, standing at the ready in front of both Roane and me, who stood by the women on horseback. One of my men licked his lips in preparation, eager to spill the blood of men of the Summer Court.

"Took you long enough," I said to Roane, a grin stretching my lips.

Roane returned the smile, adjusting his armor and looking around at the battlefield. "Figured I'd take my time, once our men got there anyhow. Bloodbath in those catacombs, Stryder. Not one left alive."

"And our men?"

"Not a scratch on them. This is what they've been waiting for. Take it right to the queen's forces. I don't think they've ever been happier or more loyal than they are right this second."

"There has to be thirty of them, but I can't see clearly because of the trees. Thirty plus a few from the group that held us off."

"And we've got, what, ten? Including you and me?" Roane asked, calculating our chances, strategizing in his brilliant mind.

"Looks that way."

"How many did we have at the Battle of Gretchet?"

Just the mention of that horrific battle was enough to spur me, to increase the anger coursing through my body. The war hadn't been kind to anyone, but I was determined it was about to get much worse for those who had threatened the people of Sidhe, especially my own people, and now Kip.

"Seventy-two."

"And how many did the Summer Court bring?" Roane asked.

"When we counted the dead, it was more than three hundred."

"Right," Roane continued, "so we should be done here in ten, twenty minutes? Early enough for supper, I'd say."

My old friend smiled at me and unsheathed his sword. My men, knowing the sound better than the voices of their own mothers, took the cue and unsheathed theirs, charging forward into the bulk of the Summer Queen's men, who still looked unprepared. We nodded to each other and then went back to back, staying back close to the women to fend off any who got around or through our ranks.

I unfurled my wings and Roane did the same, and adrenaline shot through me, my need to protect Kip combining with the brotherhood of my men and the taste for war. From behind me, I heard the sound of two more swords being unsheathed. I turned and saw Kip and Harley, swords at the ready, standing beside the horses. A part of me wanted to tell her to mount up again and wait to run, but I stopped. She wanted to protect herself, and to protect her friend. I knew that desire, and I respected it. She had shown herself shockingly capable by escaping the cell earlier and making it to where I'd found her. Perhaps she would find herself equally instinctively good in battle, should she need to wield that sword.

Whatever fatigue I had felt before Roane arrived was gone. I was ready for battle once again.

17

Kip

The men that arrived with Roane and Harley charged into the trees, swords clanging and battle cries filling the woods with the sound of bloodthirst and vengeance. I had stepped down off Thunder and Stryder looked back at me. I tried to look as imposing and prepared as possible, despite my glaring lack of training on the sword. That couldn't hold me back. I couldn't let yet another fight go by and stand around doing nothing. Especially one that seemed as dangerous as this one. I knew Stryder's men were fearsome fighters, and that they had often fought with odds heavily against them, but I still felt like being prepared to defend myself was my best bet at survival.

Maybe I could even help. The chances of that weren't spectacular, but if things started to go wrong, I'd take surviving.

When a stern look or command didn't come from Stryder, and instead he nodded and returned to standing back to back with Roane, I realized he had decided to trust me. Part of me was absolutely terrified, but another, smaller part of me was exhilarated. Something about this moment felt right. I couldn't explain it to myself, much less anyone else, but somehow I felt like this moment was meant to be. That I was doing exactly what I was supposed to be doing.

A few of the Fae made their way around Stryder's men and charged after us. Stryder met one of them head-on, and their swords slashed through the air. Two others came after Roane and he took a step back to avoid a swinging attack. The swinging swordsman stumbled and fell to the ground as Roane slashed at the other one, striking him in his shoulder and sending him flying. Stryder had made quick work of the Fae he had fought as well, and turned to me as the Fae fell to his knees and collapsed.

The thought ran through my mind a split second before I went into action. As the swordsman stood and squared up with both Roane and Stryder, his back was turned to me. Stepping forward the two steps it took to close the gap, I inexpertly kicked him as hard as I could in the back. I had half expected him to roll forward, maybe even into Stryder's waiting sword. Instead, he took barely a step forward and made a soft, muffled *oomph* sound.

Turning slowly, his eyes searched for mine and found them. A malicious smile spread across his lips and his sword raised in preparation to stab at me. Before he could thrust forward, his body suddenly went stock still. Blood pooled at the bottom of his neck and then began to run down in a hundred tiny rivulets that then became a flood. His mouth opened and a whimpering sound came out, more of a breath than a voice, and he dropped to his knees. Eyes that had looked into mine stayed staring forward as the head fell, rolling to the side and away as the body crumpled to the ground. When the head stopped rolling, I could see the eyes, still open, staring up blankly into the now darkening sky.

I expected to be horrified by the sudden display of violence, but instead, I was relieved. Stryder looked up to me and our eyes met again. I nodded at him and he spun on his heel, bracing for another attack. Several more had broken the ranks and were heading for us. Roane and Stryder each headed for them, cutting them off. A voice cried out from beside me and I turned to see a Fae grasping at Harley. She swung wildly at him, but he barely budged, moving closer to her and raising a sword. Roane was busy with two others and Stryder had his hands full with a particularly large Fae.

This was on me.

I barreled into him as best I could, swiping my sword. It only gave him a scratch, but it managed to surprise him enough that I attacked, jumping on him. We both tumbled into the ground and I lost the sword in a sea of men and horses. Rolling to my side, I saw him scramble up, his sword in the air as he aimed to slice at me. Before he could bring it down and cut me in half, a sword seemed to appear magically in his chest. The blade ran all the way out, almost curving back toward his lips, and he dropped his own, falling to his knees. As he did, the blade retracted and I could see Stryder behind him, his long, dark hair now matted to his face with sweat and scratches and small wounds littering his arms and chest. He smiled briefly at me and then was gone to fight again.

Harley rushed over and helped me up. "Thanks for saving my ass there," she said dryly.

"Oh, you know, just tackling giant Fae men with swords. My normal Tuesday," I said.

Harley laughed and then a serious expression seeped down from her eyes to the bottom of her face, as if a curtain had been dropped on a stage.

"We need to get somewhere safer. Just a few feet back, I think. Things are pretty intense here."

I nodded. I didn't want to leave the action, or Stryder, but she was right. It was much harder to hurt someone with a sword than I expected, so I was pretty useless at the moment.

We walked a short distance away, leading the horses with us, until we felt like we were hidden and safe.

It felt wrong to leave, even if I didn't know how to fight myself. Something about this battle, and the battle of Stryder's people in general, seemed to resonate deeply within me. I wondered how much Mac knew. I'd met him so young, but he seemed like he had been around forever. I remembered what the men said when I was trapped in the prison cell. Had Mac really known all along and was trying to guide me? So many things were clicking into place. The story of the two towers rang strongly in my mind. It was like Mac was subtly training me. Through telling me that story, he instilled in me that if I was ever caught, I would end up there. He gave me a map for a land that had never been mapped with those stories, silly stories I thought were nothing more than entertainment.

I was lost deep in thought, my eyes barely registering what they were seeing, when something snapped me back to reality. Stryder was fighting two men at once, and was about to dispatch both of them when a third body came from around a tree. It snuck toward him soundlessly in the chaos of the moment, and I saw the glimmer of a knife. A scream tried to well up in my throat, but it wasn't fast enough. Before I could yell his name, the figure had plunged the knife deep into Stryder's back.

Stryder let out a yell and crumpled to his knees. The man nonchalantly walked around him, pushing aside the bodies of the dead men with his feet to stand face to face with Stryder. It was the man who had led them before, the man Stryder had called Elgin.

Elgin drew a sword, an ornate longsword with a gold hilt and jewels embedded inside, and placed the blade on Stryder's shoulders. An evil smile crept across his lips and he began to swing the blade backwards. I ran forward, screaming Stryder's name as panic, rage, and fear for him rolled through my body like a tidal wave.

There was a loud sound, like a storm had landed directly over us, and an intense wind filled the forest. The wind howled and trees swayed and water began dumping down on us from somewhere above. Slipping on fresh mud, I fell to the ground. My legs slipped as I scrambled to regain my feet. I chanced a peek toward Stryder, not wanting to, but having to, expecting to see his severed head on the ground. Instead, I saw Stryder, head intact, leaning over as Elgin fought with the wind, which was seeming to try to rip the sword from his hand. He latched on to it with both hands, trying to pull it down and under control, when Stryder leapt up with his own sword, burying it into Egin's heart.

Just as suddenly as the wind and rain came, they stopped, and Elgin fell to the ground, Stryder's sword still stuck in him. Elgin tried to scratch and pull himself away, spittle streaming from his mouth and his body pouring blood. His eyes searched the woods and found mine, and he stopped where he was, reaching out his hand, mouthing words I couldn't hear. He kept crawling, as if he was determined to get to me before his last breath, but Stryder appeared behind him. Kneeling down, Stryder stopped Elgin's movements.

Pulling his head back by the chin, Stryder reached behind him and pulled the knife from his own back. He placed the dagger at one end of Elgin's throat, but Elgin's eyes had not left mine. He continued to try to speak as I shut my eyes and turned away. When I opened them again, his face was buried in wet dirt, and blood pooled by his neck. Stryder stood woozily and tossed the knife down, grabbing the hilt of his sword, and using his foot to pull the blade from Elgin's unprotesting body.

18

Stryder

Mayhem reigned in the woods as fights from deeper in the forest got louder and shouts of orders and instructions seemed to come from everywhere. Summer Fae were retreating, but my men were chasing, which left us mostly alone. Some of the Summer Fae must have waited for that moment, and came out, fresh and ready for battle, with only Roane and me to face them. And now, I had no time to consider what had just happened, how a raging magical storm had swooped in to save me just in time. These men wore different uniforms, with a plume on their helmets that at once signified importance but also served to make them look like complete buffoons. I hated plumes on helmets.

They were also a wider variety of sizes of men physically and carried a large range of weaponry. It must be a special unit, designed for this type of attack, as one of them swung a spiked chain with a ball on the end and another carried what looked like a spear that had knives attached to the wood in a circle around the main blade. The spiked ball Fae was the closest, and I rolled in a zig zag to avoid him knowing where to throw the ball. I felt it whistle by me and crash into the ground. His body yanked backward, his great arms pulling the chain and sending the ball flying in an arc back toward him. Instead of catching it, he stepped to the side and let momentum begin a new swing for the heavy weapon.

I rolled to the side, ducking and weaving, trying to judge when he was going to throw it again. From seemingly nowhere, another Fae attacked me on the side, knocking me over and forcing me to struggle with him on the ground. The pain in my back was intense, but I had to push through. The plumed helmet above me jostled as I wrenched it off the Fae's head, revealing long black hair and a scarred face. He reached up to punch me and I tried to buck him off me. Instead, the fist came down and immediately his body disappeared off of me. I looked over to see that the spiked ball had missed me, but hit him directly in the stomach, driving him into the trunk of a tree.

I scrambled to my feet as the ball and chain Fae stomped to the body it was stuck in. Taking the opportunity, I jumped on his back, dragging my sword across his throat and then slamming the point in down at an angle at his breastplate, getting under the armor and driving down straight into his guts. He tumbled down, landing hard on his own spiked ball, one long metal spike piercing his eye.

Before I could pull my sword out from him, another Fae was on me, and I threw him hard into a tree. As soon as his feet hit the ground, I was on him, landing punches to his sides and crunching his ribs. I saw the knife being pulled from its sheath and seized his arm, bending it toward him and breaking it as I forced him to stab himself. I ripped off the helmet and used it to pummel him in the face until his body slumped over. The pain was becoming overwhelming and I leaned on the tree for support as I caught a moment to breathe. Roane was fighting valiantly just a few feet from me and I steeled myself, grabbing the hilt of my sword and yanking on it until it was free of the large Fae's body.

Just before I could reach Roane, I heard the yells from behind me, and I turned to see three Fae men approaching Harley and Kip. I bolted for the area, the fatigue and pain being pushed to the back of my mind, and used what little magical ability I had left to force my wings to catch air as I leapt, allowing me to drop down onto the men in one movement. Two of them crashed together as the third rolled away. My sword found flesh on one of the men and ripped his side apart before I put my feet down to the ground and focused on the other. He was still on the ground, trying to get up, and I shoved the sword down into his back, effectively staking him into the ground. I turned my attention to the third Fae, who was standing now, a knife in his hand and Kip in front of him.

"She's coming with me, Stryder," the Fae said, grabbing at Kip and pulling her close to him.

"Not if I still breathe," I growled, feeling the rage empty me, building the strength for one more magical blast. There might not be much left after I did it, but there was no stopping it now.

"She comes with me or she dies. She's just a human, Stryder."

"She is not just a human," I growled. "She is so much more."

The words had come out before I could stop them. Kip's face screwed up in confusion and the Fae behind her began to howl with laughter. It was a mirthless laugh, of sarcasm and hatred and opportunity. He had just seen a way to make himself a legend, and his knife began to speed toward Kip's neck. My hand shot out in an instant, and a blue-green blast exploded out of my palm, hitting his hand with the knife, his face behind it, several trees and another Fae in the distance, and creating a hole in each.

The suddenly faceless Fae dropped to the ground and Kip ran to me, embracing me for a moment. I wanted to stay in that embrace, hold her to me while the world around us fell, to tell her what everything meant, but instead I just shook my head and pulled her away. Our enemies were still near.

That didn't stop her curiosity. "You said I was so much more. What does that even mean?"

"You're my Fated Mate." The words fell from my lips, unbidden and unrestrained. I hadn't intended to tell her. Especially not now, when we were still in danger. But when I looked into her eyes and felt her body curled so familiarly against mine, nothing would stop the words. It was as if it wasn't really me speaking, but the words coming out of my heart to find their way into hers. I'd been holding them back for so long, I couldn't do it anymore.

Kip gasped, the confusion in her eyes only deepening as she tried to process the unknown phrase. "I don't understand what that means, but it sounds... complicated."

"I'll explain later," I told her.

The stream of Fae began to thin and as I joined Roane again, we continued on. In the distance I could hear the battle slowing down there too, and only hoped that our forces had created the path we needed. As the last of the plumed battalion hit the ground, blood soaking the trees so much it looked like autumn had come early, Roane knelt to the ground to catch his breath. I did the same as the women and the horses met us in the clearing.

"You're hurt, Stryder," Roane said.

"I know," I said, then noticed Kip behind me. "I'm fine. Just need to get through this battle and on to somewhere safe."

"We have a place, not far from here. It's where our men hid. Less than a day's ride," Roane continued.

"Good. Let's check the men," I said, standing shakily.

I was grateful for Thunder being there beside me as I grabbed his reins to steady myself. He nuzzled into my neck and I pat him under his chin. Turning, I noticed Kip was a little way off, wrapping something up in a large blanket. I motioned to her when her attention returned to me, telling her to mount him.

"No, Stryder, please, you are hurt. You need to get on the horse," she said, stuffing whatever she had wrapped in a bag at Thunder's side.

"I'd feel more comfortable if you were on Thunder. Just in case more of them are still around," I said, waving my sword in the general direction of the woods. "I need to know Thunder can take you to safety."

Without arguing again, she mounted, and we began to make our way through the dense woods. After a mile or so of littered dead Fae bodies, we came upon a small semi-circle of our men. Four stood, leaning against their swords as they waited. They hopped up and stood at attention when they saw me arrive and the eldest one, Balor, spoke.

"King, we have defeated their forces, but they have sent for yet more reinforcements. While we would revel in the fight, sir, the cargo must be delivered safely."

"Seriously? Cargo?" Kip began but I interrupted her.

"She is not cargo. She is quite possibly the key to winning this damned war. But yes, Balor, we must go. I have heard you have a hidden place nearby."

"Yes, my lord," he said, bowing. "We will escort you there and ensure your safety. The horses," he shouted, turning to his men. They scattered into the woods, each whistling a different tune, and suddenly seven horses arrived.

"There are seven. But only five of you," Roane said to Balor.

"Yes. One has gone to bring news back to our court. The other has perished in glory, sir."

"Who?" I asked.

"Anderson, sir. He was a good brother and died valiantly."

Balor pounded his fist on his chest twice and bowed his head. Roane and I repeated the salute.

"His body?" I asked.

"Already with the messenger, sir. Now we must leave, the night grows dark."

I nodded and two of the men fell back behind us as the other three forged ahead. After a while, Kip slipped out of the saddle and motioned for me to come close.

"I have something for you, I just thought you should have it," she said meekly.

"What is it?" I asked as she rummaged into the bag, pulling out the wrapped item she had put in earlier.

She handed it to me carefully and I unwrapped it, marveling at what was before me.

It was the most beautiful sword I had ever seen. The hilt was gold, encrusted in smooth, creamy-colored stones and bright jewels. The blade was sharp and it was perfectly balanced. It must have been enchanted as well, as its lightness suggested I held a feather, but I could tell its cutting power could go through bone as easily as water. I recognized it and looked into Kip's eyes. I would have to explain everything to her very soon. For her to have gotten this for me from the battlefield meant her feelings were growing stronger. She needed to understand what existed between us.

I swallowed painfully at the thought, knowing the complications that would soon cause.

"It was the man you called Elgin's. I get the feeling that a man like that wouldn't appreciate its beauty. He didn't deserve a sword like this; it looks better suited for a king," she said, her gaze intense. "Besides, you earned it."

I smiled at her and unsheathed my own trusty sword. I'd had it since my youth, rejecting any other sword offered more fit for a king. But to receive a gift like this from my own mate, I couldn't reject it. It was an honor to receive this gift. Placing my old sword in the sheath on the side of Thunder, I slid the new one into place on my side. It felt light, and yet powerful. It felt right.

19

Kip

What I just experienced was so dizzying, I wasn't totally aware of what was going on around me. The movement of Ominous Thunder beneath me ensured I knew we were moving forward, but part of me was still on that battlefield. It wasn't just the intensity of the fighting or the blood and dirt that covered me. It wasn't even the first feeling of the sword in my hand and the sense of power and strength I got from even my small part of the fight. What Stryder told me was pounding heavily in the back of my mind.

Fated Mates. Those were the words he'd used. As in, fate. I didn't fully understand the revelation, but he'd said it with such determination and seriousness I knew it meant something significant. It felt like something he'd been holding back from me for a long time, kept hidden away so he didn't have to face it. Maybe so neither of us did. Just hearing the words in the memory of his voice was enough to send a shiver along my skin and make my heart skip a beat. It wasn't an obscure term. Unless I was completely off base and this was one of those Land of Sidhe things that seemed like one thing and actually turned out to be something completely different, of course.

But I doubted it was. The way Stryder's eyes stared into mine when he said them, the way those words linked together so much of what had already happened between us, I knew what they meant. Maybe not specifically. Maybe not in the exact context of his world. But I understood they meant we were fated to be together. Somehow, we had been bonded to one another even before we knew the other existed.

I was going to go ahead and put a pin in that topic so we could revisit later. That was going to need some elaboration.

As much as it gnawed at me, there was still a voice inside that questioned whether I could truly trust Stryder. Even after everything we'd been through, I couldn't escape the reality that I didn't understand him or his world yet. In so many ways I was on the outside, watching what was unfolding and still trying to get a grasp on it. There was an unavoidable possibility that I was still being manipulated and would soon be handed over to the wizards and sacrificed.

But that was only a small part of me. The rest had watched the way Stryder fought and seen the passion in his eyes. He had given his body over and willingly accepted the pain and brutality if it meant protecting me and continuing on in his mission. A man who wasn't trustworthy and honorable wouldn't do that.

It seemed like we traveled for days after the battle without the sun setting, but Roane kept reassuring us we were getting close. Finally, a shape in the distance began to look more solid. It turned from just a vague outline into what looked like a pile of rocks against the side of a hill, like a landslide had deposited them there some unknown time ago. We got down off the horses and the men went to work detaching all the bags and supplies. Stryder's movements were slow and painful, but he grit his teeth and said nothing. He did as much work as Roane, possibly even more, as though he needed to prove to himself and everyone around us that he was still strong, that the Summer Fae hadn't destroyed him.

They led Harley and me around to the side of the pile of rocks. The other men gathered close behind as Roane pushed one of the stones away. It moved far more easily under his hand than it looked like it would and I realized this was a concealed shelter. We ducked inside and found ourselves in what I could only describe as a cave. It didn't seem to have been carved out naturally, but crafted by someone or something. There was more than enough space for them to pile up our bags and then Roane pointed into the darkness beyond the light filtering into the first chamber.

"There are rooms that way," he said. "Food, other supplies. We can stay here until we recover."

He used a flint from the pouch at his hip to light two torches. One he handed to Harley and the other he offered to me. I took it and used my other arm to link through Stryder's so I could guide him into one of the rooms. His eyes locked on the bath against the far wall like it was the greatest thing he had ever seen. After using the torch to light another attached to the wall, I dipped out of the room and went back to the main room for some of our bags. I expected to find the other warriors, or at least Harley and Roane still there, but they were gone, all apparently drawn to the promise of bathing and sleep as much as Stryder.

When I got back into the room, Stryder was submerged in the deep tub. The soap he was using to scrub himself foamed lavishly, filling the tub with bubbles as he went. That was something I could definitely get used to. Instant bubble bath. And Stryder in it. The water glistened on his golden skin, accentuating the cut of his muscles. He had loosened his hair and dipped back into the water to wet it. It hung around his face and clung to his skin. I had the urge to run my fingers through it and feel the strands against my skin. Wings drooping, hanging to his side, he looked up at me as I unpacked one of the bags.

"What are you doing?" he asked.

"I don't think you can wait for Minerva to get all the way out here, so I'm going to take care of your injuries," I told him.

He looked like he was getting ready to protest, then gave an almost imperceptible nod. "Thank you," he murmured.

When I had everything I needed, I knelt down by the tub and used a cloth to dry the wounds I could see. Using materials we'd gathered earlier from our journey and a few things Minerva had evidently snuck into our supplies before we left her house, I tended to each of Stryder's injuries. It took everything in me to keep my eyes focused above the surface of the water. My heart fluttered with the heat and tension building in the room. It felt like forever since we'd been alone together and my awareness of it being just the two of us got more intense with every moment.

I let my fingertips trail along the muscles of his arms as I wrapped his wounds, then traced his chiseled chest and belly as I carefully covered a wide scrape in his side. After a few minutes, his hand came down to slowly wrap around my wrist. My breath shuddered from between my lips as my eyes slowly rose to meet his.

"What I told you earlier," he said. "I want you to understand how important that is."

"What does it mean?" I asked. "Are we really…destined to be together?"

Stryder gave a long, slow nod. "Yes. It is a very special bond, but for now it needs to stay between us."

That qualification fell strangely hard and painful into my stomach. "Why?"

Stryder moved his hand down to take mine. "There was a time when Fated Mates were what was expected. Virtually all

Fae found their mates and built their lives around each other. As time passed, these bonded relationships became fewer and farther between. In my lifetime, they have faded into obscurity. They are very rare now, to the point that some don't even believe they exist anymore. But they do." He stared into my eyes and I felt like I could fall into them forever. "You and me, we were crafted to be together, made to spend our lives together."

"Is that why you couldn't kill me?" I asked.

I knew Stryder was devoted to his people and would do whatever he could to protect them, but keeping me alive was a tremendous risk. This was the only explanation that made sense.

"Yes," he said, drawing my hand closer to his chest. "I couldn't do it. The moment I saw you, I knew there was something special about you. It drew me to you and wouldn't let me go. When I realized you are my Fated Mate, it changed everything for me. You are so much more than a part of this war, Kip. You are my life."

My hand pressed to his chest and I could feel the tremble of his heart. We leaned toward each other, pulled to one another, and our mouths met. The kiss was cautious at first, like we were testing the closeness. But that small taste was too much to ignore. Instantly, I needed more of him. I moaned, leaning forward and Stryder's tongue parted my lips. Hunger and longing filled my chest that only Stryder's caresses would fill. I suddenly had to have more.

Brushing the tools in my lap onto the ground, I rose up onto my knees to be closer to him. Stryder shifted and wrapped one arm around my waist, his hand fisting in the bunches of my skirt. The water from the bath soaked through my clothes, but I didn't care. That heat was nothing compared to what was sizzling in my chest and low in my belly. My fingers dug through the thick black hair spilling down his shoulders and along his back. Our kiss deepened and the sound of his wings stretching heightened my response to him.

There was something wild and savage about the way he gripped me close, the way his mouth devoured mine, the way his hardness pressed into my stomach. I wanted to know every inch of Stryder's skin, to see and feel and touch and taste, to kiss and never stop, to live and breathe this man.

I was nearly climbing into the tub when the door to the room burst open and I jerked back in surprise. The men coming in stumbled over apologies as I scrambled away from Stryder and he glared at them fiercely. "What is it?" he barked, his voice gruff.

"I'm sorry, sir," one said. "We were concerned about the condition of your injuries, especially after you didn't come into the kitchen for food, and we came to check on you."

Stryder's eyes continued to carve into them for a few more seconds before his shoulders relaxed slightly. "Thank you for your concern," he said. "Kip has tended to my injuries and they should heal fine. I'll go to eat soon."

The men nodded and scurried out of the room, trying hard to keep their eyes averted from me.

"Wow," I said, brushing hair away from my burning cheeks.

"I'm sorry," he said.

I shook my head. "No, it's all right. It's good that you have men who are so loyal and care about you so much."

Stryder reached for my hand again and I stepped forward, taking in a deep breath as I gave it to him. He frowned and I knew I wasn't going to like what he was about to say.

"And it's because of them, because of everything that's happening, that we shouldn't let ourselves get distracted."

I knew what he meant and knew he was right, though I couldn't help the disappointment clawing at my chest. I tried to be honorable, like him. "I agree. Our relationship shouldn't be our focus right now. We need to get you back to the Blood Court and bring an end to this war."

It's the right thing, I told myself. But even as I said it, my chest clenched. All I wanted to do was focus on him. But that wasn't why I was there. My true purpose had to come first. Right?

20

*S*tryder

The incline of the hill was steep but we forced our way up anyway. My back was beginning to feel almost normal again and the pain in the scrapes and cuts along my body had dulled until I almost didn't notice them. Over the last two days spent camped in the hidden shelter, my energy had returned. We'd made impressive progress and I could feel us getting closer to the Blood Court, to my home.

I looked to my right and saw Kip and Harley chatting with one another, almost as if they hadn't just spent the last few days traveling through a warzone. Kip had grown so much in just a short time, going from a timid, scared young woman to someone who knew her abilities and knew that they were growing. Knew that she belonged.

Ahead of us, Balor and two other men of mine led the way. Balor was leading them, allowing me to hang back and give him instructions to delegate to the men. He was a fine soldier, and one day would make a great general, but for now he operated best in a select group like he was in now. The elite fighters, and my most trusted men. I'd take six of them against a thousand of any other army any day.

Roane walked alone, just behind all of us, his eyes wide and piercing, looking for any sign of danger from behind us. As usual, Roane had my back, and I could trust him to make sure no surprises were coming. I couldn't help but notice, though, that every once in a while his gaze would slow down considerably. It always seemed to be just as it passed over Harley. I had known Roane for a long time, and this was as fixated on any woman as I had ever seen him. I worried at first that it would distract him, but instead it seemed to make him stronger. His talent on the battlefield in the woods was more evident than I had ever seen it, and I knew he would be fine. I also knew a little about how women could make a man fight harder.

Thunder walked beside me, my trusty steed, and I patted him gently on the neck. When we had crested this hill and reached the valley, we would truly be in the Realm of the Blood Court. There, I would give him a long rest and some more of the treats Kip had found for them. He deserved them. I'd ridden him as little as possible, knowing how exhausted he was, and I looked forward to rewarding him as much as I could.

Those treats would come soon as the hill's incline slowly leveled off, and we stood at the top, looking down over a much softer, lazier decline into the realm. The Blood Court lay in the distance with only a stretch of fertile but tattered land between us and our final goal.

Kip and Harley, who had been lost in a conversation, stopped and stared out over the lands before us. They were lush and green and water flowed from a river that led to the foot of the hill. Two of my men went ahead, down the hill to check out the area before we settled.

"I think we can make an early camp by the riverside," I said. "Let the horses rest and cook a nice meal."

"And maybe a bath," Harley blurted out. Roane's wide eyes

snapped to her and she immediately turned red, a smile stretching wide across her face as she stumbled over a few sounds I could only assume were supposed to be words.

"Yes," I interrupted, hoping to save her some embarrassment, "a nice long swim will do us all good. The waters here are said to be healing."

"How is your wound, Stryder?" Kip said, stepping close to me and leaving Harley to start counting grass or find intricate shapes in clouds or whatever she could do to not make eye contact with Roane again.

"It's doing fine. Sore. The water will wash away any infection, and I can get it stitched up if it isn't healing fast enough. Balor is a master at sewing up wounds," I said. Kip made a face like she just had a vivid image of Balor's fingers working their way around needles and string and skin.

"Great. That's great," she said, trying to conceal her distaste.

We walked along in silence for a few moments, taking in the change of air and scenery, and Kip closed the gap between us so we were walking close enough to brush against each other, and my arm tingled every time it happened. She was about to say something when I spoke.

"So, I have something for you," I said.

She turned to me, surprised, then raised her eyebrow. "Oh yeah?" I could tell by the way her lips twitched that she was trying to suppress a smile.

"I'll show you when we set up camp."

I could also tell that she didn't want to wait, but she was willing to for me. I still hadn't decided exactly what I would say when I gave it to her, and I was trying to find just the right words. I hoped they would come to me when I got there. We made our way down the incline and I noticed the two scouts had not returned yet. I walked up to Balor and Roane joined me.

"Where are the other men? Has there been trouble?" I asked.

"No, my lord. If there had been trouble, undoubtedly either

one would have returned or they would have created smoke to alert us."

"You guys really need some cell towers in this place," Harley grumbled, stopping next to Kip.

After a confused pause and laughter from Kip, Balor continued. "Wherever they are they are either alone, or with peaceful people. If I may hazard a guess, sir?" Balor asked. I nodded. "I would guess there are villagers here. We are on the outskirts of the Blood Court, but this area is valued for its crops, not its strategic positioning. There has been damage and bloodshed, but the battles here aren't frequent."

"Our men are probably just reassuring them of your return," Roane suggested.

I nodded, and they both walked away, but something still didn't feel right. Calling Roane back over, I pulled him close so no one else could hear.

"Something's wrong. I will make camp. Be focused and vigilant watching for our men or any villagers," I said.

Roane gave a curt nod and walked over to Balor. I heard him say something about firewood, and Balor saluted before walking over to the horses to begin setting up camp. When everything was set, and the fire had been started, I took Kip aside to Thunder.

"I want you to have this," I said. "It isn't as pretty as the one you gave me, but it will serve you well. This way, I am always with you."

I unwrapped my own sword, with its cut diamond in the shape of my family's sigil in the hilt, and presented it to her. Her face was awash in surprise as she took it tenderly from my hands. She gripped it tightly, stepping away from me and taking an experimental swing. As she did, something inside of me twinged, and a feeling washed over me that what I saw before me wasn't just my Fated Mate, but was something more. Destiny. Her brandishing my sword was destiny. I had once been the king of a realm of peace, but now was merely the King of Ashes. But if I had her by my side, perhaps... Perhaps destiny would be kinder than that. I could find something in the ashes again.

She carefully lowered the sword to her side and I stepped up close to her, running my fingers along the side of her face.

"Balor, Stryder, they are here," Roane began in a cheerful tone, but his voice then dropped and he shouted back to me, "Stryder, it's the wizards."

I ran back to the camp with Kip close behind me. The arrival of the wizards was unexpected and that made my throat tighten and my stomach feel heavy. It was very unlikely they were here to greet me happily and welcome me home.

They were walking toward Roane and Harley just as I ran back into the camp. I positioned myself between them and Kip, pushing her toward the rest of the group to make her less vulnerable.

"King," the lead wizard said, bowing his head and putting his fist to his heart in the traditional gesture of respect for his king.

"Greyfeld," I acknowledged.

"What is she doing here?" he demanded angrily, raising one finger to point toward Kip.

"She is here with me," I said defiantly.

"You were sent to destroy her."

"Plans changed."

The men came down from their horses and approached us. I refused to step back.

"Did we not make the prophecy clear to you, Stryder?" Greyfeld asked in a low, rumbling tone.

"Your prophecy was clear," I told him.

"Then this ends here. Kill her."

I straightened my spine and stared at him, unflinching even as I felt the muscles in my jaw twitch and spasm with the buildup of tension and anger forming there. This man was meant to be one I could entrust with everything, in whose hands I could lay my life and feel secure. Now he was standing in front of me trying to tear my very soul from within me and expecting me to offer it up without question. It infuriated me that he would not only ask that of me, but to force it on me like he was the one in control.

"Step down."I bellowed. "Do not forget I am still your king. I will do as I please."

"What you please will bring an end to our world. She shouldn't be here. Destroy her or we will do it for you."

I glanced over my shoulder and saw Kip with my sword tight in her hands, held above her head as she braced herself to fight.

A smile flickered across my lips and I turned to face the wizards.

Copyright © 2019 by Ava Mason

All rights reserved.

No part of this book may be reproduced in any form or by any electronic or mechanical means, including information storage and retrieval systems, without written permission from the author, except for the use of brief quotations in a book review.

Made in United States
North Haven, CT
10 March 2023